The
HOUSEBOAT
VERONICA

The
HOUSEBOAT
VERONICA

A Novel

Josh Bell

TUSCALOOSA

Copyright © 2024 by Josh Bell
The University of Alabama Press
Tuscaloosa, Alabama 35487-0380
All rights reserved

FC2 is an imprint of the University of Alabama Press

Inquiries about reproducing material from this work should be addressed to
the University of Alabama Press

Book Design: Publications Unit, Department of English, Illinois State
    University; Director: Steve Halle, Production Intern: Gwen Johnson
Cover design: Matthew Revert
Typeface: Adobe Jenson Pro

Library of Congress Cataloging-in-Publication Data is available from the
Library of Congress.

ISBN: 978-1-57366-204-8
E-ISBN: 978-1-57366-906-1

CONTENTS

—

TIMELINE

—

This was the time of one moon and one sun and one sky, the time of the oncoming apocalypse which still wasn't coming, the time of vampire moths and of the hairlessness of men and stars, the time before the Empaths, the time of puncture, the time of four seasons to the year (Summer 1, Summer 2, Summer 3, and sometimes Winter), the time of the Great Pornographies, the time of the sun like a giant head searching the ditch of the earth for its body, the time before the human colonies of Mars and the time before time travel, the time of cherry pits and purses, the time of the black-haired woman and the black-haired woman, still the time when the calendar could make you pregnant.

THE BLACK-HAIRED WOMAN

—

She said things like "Everyone wants to belong to a witch," and "A name is a carnivorous animal." Her penmanship lifted off and vibrated. She had incredibly long toes and she'd killed a lot of people.

—

In this life (and perhaps others) she'd been called murderer and pimp. She'd been called Freak-Witch and Hard Woman and Candlestick and Mrs. Sometimes and Nancy-Witch and Creepwitch and Cupcake, Tom-Witch and half and half and Superwitch and Mistress Forobosco and Knife-Wife and the Green Witch and Tiptoe Killer and White Witch and Girl-Unit and Fish Doctor.

She'd been called bad names and all names and some names I won't repeat and names no one else had been called.

She'd been called too many names and she kept track of these names, kept track of them with a scrupulousness.

For there on the houseboat *Veronica*, beneath the huge white bed in the black-haired woman's sleeping quarters, lurked a batwing-bound black book, a book into which she'd written every bad name she'd been called in her life.

—

I say what I say knowing I'll be envied. I say it having learned the difference between being flirted with and murdered. I lived with this witch who was the black-haired woman. I lived on the houseboat *Veronica* (and didn't remember living elsewhere) and I'd seen the batwing-bound book.

It was the book of bad names. It was a considerable book.

If you had the fortune to open this book, you'd see all the names the black-haired woman had been called, logged there in her vibrating penmanship, a keeping of account. Sometimes in that book you'd see a bad name with a black line drawn through it. Some of the bad names had thick black lines drawn through them, I'm saying, though some of them did not.

—

"And the bad names with black lines drawn through them?" I asked the black-haired woman.

I asked her this, probably knowing I asked about death. For this is how it goes with most witch conversation, a proclamation, a poke in the ribs, a story, a little touch of the grave. We lay on the white bed of her sleeping quarters, head to foot, afternoon light in her spiny teeth, I with the book of bad names balanced on my chest, she with her huge black hair a void against the headboard, the invisible engines of the houseboat *Veronica* rumbling beneath us.

"Like which name?" the black-haired woman asked.

"Pond-Witch," I said, touching the page and the name with my finger, closing my eyes, trying not to let the hum of her penmanship distract me. She sat there against the headboard, lifting up her feet one by one, looking at the long shadow of her toes on the wall. With her left foot she cast the shadow of a bunny rabbit. With her right foot she cast the shadow of the wolf coming to eat it. It was weird how the wolf and the rabbit were the same size and I said to her, up from the book of bad names, "I don't think Pond-Witch is such a bad name to be called."

"Hearing the story might help," the black-haired woman said. She stopped the shadow play of her feet and blew a heavy feather of black hair from her eyes. As always it was hard for me, due to the black of her hair and how it soaked up the light, to make out her face. She said oratorically, "A young man on the deck of a shrimp trawler anchored off one of the domed island cities of the East a million years ago once called me Pond-Witch."

"What cities are the domed cities of the East?" I asked.

She shushed me. "I was young then," she said. "He called me this name in front of his friends. If he'd said such a name gently, or whispered it into my ear when we were alone together with a bottle of wine and the stars all over him, it would have been otherwise. But it wasn't otherwise. I'd thought him a kind boy. He sometimes cried when I undressed him. He was a kind boy, I think, but he also wasn't. He just stood there with his friends as witness and called me the name he called me. I had a corkscrew in one hand and a bottle of wine in the other." She let her foot drift toward me and poked me in the ribs with it. The toes felt like tines. "So I broke the bottle over his head," she said, "and then I used the corkscrew on his belly button."

THE BLACK-HAIRED WOMAN II

—

The black-haired woman had been called many names, but I'd never know her given name, or even if she'd been given a given name at all, nor where she'd come from, nor truly if she had been born. She was ancient. She drank too much benzene. When she was drunk she moved like a girl.

"Did I ever call you a name like that?" I asked, thinking of the boy with the uncorked belly button. "A name," I said, "like in the book of bad names?"

She said, "You've never called me any name at all."

—

When she stood on tiptoe, you could be certain she held a knife in her hand.

When she held a knife in her hand, you knew she stood on tiptoe.

Her hair was black and her come was pink, most likely with spells in it, all glitter and truth and ash.

The first time I saw it, pink on my stomach, I had to invent the word "love."

—

We'd sit side by side, in the heat of Summers 1, 2, and 3, the black-haired woman and I, we'd sit up on the open-air balcony deck of the houseboat *Veronica*, maybe talking about Winter, wondering if Winter might ever come. We'd sit side by side, on two cute-set pink deck chairs, the moon like a lost shoe on the black sky to the South, or I'd think it was the South, maybe the North, I in my uniform of pink knee-length shorts, the black-haired woman small aside from the pile of black hair on her head, she always-bare-of-foot and wearing the pretty green dress in the heartbreak-cut, the dress I hardly ever saw her without. This was before I'd invented the word "love," but the germ of that word already smoked inside me, plus whatever the word "murder" was, walking on stilts in my chest. I wanted to kneel before her, her smaller and older than I would be forever, to kneel and watch her lift her dress.

The heartbreak-cut green dress made her look like a paper doll, small, trim in all of two dimensions.

She looked like a paper doll, then she'd look at you like a paper doll never did.

—

"Do you remember your parents?"

This was one night. This was the black-haired woman.

"No," I said.

"Will you be my biographer?" she asked.

"All right," I said.

"Even knowing," she said, "that I come back from the dead to murder my biographer?"

"Okay," I said.

—

It seems important, beyond pointing out the moon, to say that it was night.

"I'm just kidding about the biographer thing." She was playful when she most seemed dangerous. She tilted up my face to underline the importance of what she said. Her hair made her top-heavy in her chair, all balanced uneasily over the thin skeleton, so that, along with the drunkenness, you feared she'd tip over and fall. The glint of the moon off her toenails put me in the mind of fish scales. She said, "I don't ever want to see you writing anything."

"You won't," I said seriously.

"Seriously," she said, "the last thing we need is a lot of written testament laying around."

—

The black-haired woman, whose arms and legs were thin and pale as candles, who was not a pirate but a witch, who carried in the pockets of her heartbreak-cut green dress a pink-handled suit knife with a shrunken babyfoot charm dangling from the handle, this black-haired woman was also a practiced hand at carpentry.

The balcony deck of the houseboat *Veronica* was a lovely balcony deck.

Here it was, the balcony deck: all around its four sides ran a graceful mercury railing, brazierwood slats for flooring, slats notched and sistered by the black-haired woman, hard and white as a candle in hand and foot. At each corner of the mercury balcony railing, a light pole that went up eight feet and cast down gentle light, then a little tomato garden in one corner, framed by salvaged boat wreckage. A table with an umbrella, brave and white. The two cute-set pink deck chairs, the black-haired woman and no one else alive, pink moths hovering around her head, the moon, the word "balcony" in my mouth.

—

On the balcony deck in such an atmosphere, I wanted to go down on the black-haired woman, as I have said one thousand times (and in other testament), to show her I was not afraid of the pink-handled knife with the babyfoot charm dangling from it, to show her I'd learned well from the Great Pornographies, that I was not one of those creatures who worried too much about where the next breath came from.

I wanted to prove I was a different boy than the one who'd called her Pond-Witch.

Most people are not careful when they speak. Most people don't imagine that a witch has feelings.

—

"Do you know what parents are?" she asked, pink moths hovering in the balcony light about her hair, pink moths lighting on it, tracing it with pink wing dust, her hair which was the death of combs. I forgot her question as I looked at these moths, chubby like fruit. They seemed to be born in her hair, to crawl forth from it and take wing.

"It makes me self-conscious," the black-haired woman said, "when you stare at the moths of my hair like that."

"I'm sorry," I said.

She settled in her chair, pointed her invisible face at mine.

She said, "Sooner or later they'll drink your blood, and won't that be something?"

"The moths?" I asked.

She shook her head yes. "Soon," she said, "but not quite yet."

—

Nor do I want anyone thinking that at some point in this telling the thing called parents will be revealed, or that parents are important. Parents will not be revealed, nor do they lurk, nor will nothing of a history be discovered. I lived with a witch on a boat. I will be revealed in body and maybe have my blood consumed by moths. I came (as if from nowhere) to the houseboat *Veronica*. I sit now in a cute-set pink deck chair, having certain feelings I cannot name, looking at the circus-shadow of the black-haired woman's long-toed feet.

I ride upon the houseboat *Veronica*, I say, a boat which is the present.

And I knew that the black-haired woman, who was older than I by two planets laid side by side, would tell me what parents were if she wanted me to know, pink moth shooting out at me, as if from her mouth, like it was a one-word language.

—

I hadn't been alive very often or long, but I was alive then.

"What year is it?" she would sometimes ask.

"It's the Year of the Moth," I'd say.

And she'd say, "No, it is the Year of the Nipple," or she'd say "No, it is the Year of Children's Cemeteries," or "No, it is the Year of the Month."

—

Once it was, if I remember correctly, the Year of the Nipple for three straight years.

And though it was uncertain, still, what a year could be, I enjoyed smelling the black-haired woman's hair when we sat together, side by side, the night breeze blowing through her hair, licorice and lemon and the heat of living algae, thinking about her long-toed feet, thinking of her going up on tiptoe.

"Your mother was a small domesticated animal," the black-haired woman said. "Your father is a word," she continued, "buried somewhere near the word 'mother.'"

And another night: "I ate your parents in a stew."

—

What did I know about the body in the time of one moon and one sun and one sky?

Love or hand-holding or the black-haired woman spitting cherry pits into your mouth so that something had to grow in you, even if you were a boy, it was all coming for me like a wolf on more than four legs, as I supposed it, perhaps the general fashion of her lovemaking, you or whichever body bent like wire over railing and furnishing, you and you and (yes) you, pink moths raining out of the black hair and down onto your body, crawling across your chest and back perhaps, how was I to know, or how I was a boy with visions of the future, face slaps with her hard hand—what else could it be?—and the vividness of having your genitalia described very accurately, her foreplay of showing you the Great Pornographies, which pornography for her being photos of young men like myself (or yourself) having sex with expensive leather purses (such photos dotted the interior walls of the houseboat *Veronica*, in the galley, in the cockpit, in her sleeping quarters), you sleeping next to her if she invited you to sleep with her, sleeping next to her like sleeping next to a radioactive white rod in a huge black wig which was not a wig at all, what must it be like, sheet over your head, again as I supposed it, so that the black-haired woman could take the body without the head on it.

I was a virgin then. In some ways, I am a virgin forever.

—

Innocence is not the original state. Sometimes you have to climb up to it. This much I knew. That, and sometimes you felt, looking at the sun reflected off her unpainted toenails, that it was this lovemaking and hand-holding you were hungry for, but sometimes you looked at the black-haired woman's hair and it made you hungry for something else, hungry for light, I think. The black-haired woman's black hair was so black it sucked in the available light and you couldn't really tell what her face looked like. It was hard to be familiar with her, to her. I could *not* have drawn her face from memory. Maybe it was just me. Maybe it was her face you were hungry for, I was hungry for. I'd known her all the years of my life, whatever the number of those years had lately been amounting to, and all I knew was that the black-haired woman had two eyes and, I believe, right there more or less in the center of her face, a single nose.

And also that her two eyes were black in color, black like tunnels leading into the center of whatever she was thinking, thinking about anything, thinking about you.

—

Nights on the balcony deck she drank benzene grandly, smoked giant conical cigarettes, home-rolled, pink rolling paper, thin and flexible like skin, translucent, so through the paper you could see the live things wrapped up in there, the live things which were little feelered white bugs who were its curious tobacco, burning alive.

On a night much like this she tapped her two big toes together, three times. The whorled bottoms of her feet read like a dirty map to get you from one vortex to the next. She blew a plume of smoke between her feet. The smoke of her living cigarette smelled like pine and leather. She stood up in her small body—for she was very small, a toy witch—and moved her chair so that she'd put her feet in my lap, relax while she waited on me to answer her question about parents.

Her toes were long enough you imagined she could weave a blanket with them.

I looked up from her toes to the moon, and in its frost of light, a pack of white bats came diving, small moons in formation, toward the school of pink moths just now hovering around the black-haired woman's hair, one white bat snapping like a turtle, another bat veering off.

(How I wanted to sleep beneath the blanket her long toes had woven.)

"You're my parents," I said to her.

"That's what you're likely to say," she said. She was patient. She said, in her voice which was both soft and hard, low and high, singing harmony with itself, "I really don't think you know what parents are."

—

"Shoes are coming for all of us," she said, low and high, in meditation. She drug from the rustling pink cigarette and took a swig from the bottle of benzene she kept near her at all times. I never saw her with shoes. Possibly I never saw her sober, bruises spotted up and down the candle legs.

Neither was I very sure she had been born.

She had a belly button, yes.

Not that that proves anything. The world is full of trickery and craft.

Sometimes I imagined myself small enough to run the inside loop of her belly button, as if it were a wheel.

—

She looked up at the moon and one by one, like the little wolves they were, the white bats came flying in formation, taking turns on her hair, plinking off moths from the cloud of pink moths hovering around it, emerging from it. She was herself, but she was also this system, connecting the wilds to the engine, the boat to the moon. The boat chugged along, going I never knew where, maybe North and South simultaneously. I was just beginning to know the difference between port and starboard. The black-haired woman piloted the boat with her mind, or so she told me. She said how in her mind she told the stars where the *Veronica* was and the *Veronica* where the stars were. She shot out the anchor directly from her heart. I didn't question it. I wouldn't have known how. She piloted the *Veronica* with her mind, so be it. A witch, she did not lack magic. And now she let her eyes roll back into her head and the chortle of the boat engines changed to a chuckle and the boat began to move on an arc it hadn't been moving on before, like dancing.

"Simply put," she said, "your parents handed you to me. I put money in your father's hand. Your father took you from your mother and your father handed you to me. They were your mother and your father and those are what we know as parents. Though in some ways," she said, "and this is where it gets confusing, your father was your mother, and my money was your father. I put my money in your father's hand," she said, seeming to see this action rising up before her, her own hand floating out at me, "and then your father gave you to me, like as if you were born, born to me from his hand, and this was very lucky for you." She put her hand, that part of her which had given birth to me, on my shoulder. She looked around the flat blackness of the lake, some point of land jabbing at us accusingly from the dark. She trailed off. When she started talking again she wasn't talking about parents anymore but something worse. "We weren't the first people to live here, you know," she said. She wiggled her toes. She clutched her heartbreak-cut green dress around her knees. "There were people here before us, in hats and having bills to pay, and there were even people before those people, and before that even. At some point, yes, we came along. We needed the room so we murdered everyone." She said the word "we" like it was her and me, personally, who'd done this murdering. "We murdered everyone," she said, "and now we do get lonely, you and I."

DESCRIPTION BY MOTHLIGHT

—

"Stand up and let me describe you," she said.

—

I took off the pink shorts and folded them neatly, as I had been taught, the rock of the boat, the warm wind on my skin. Winter seemed a long way off, maybe nowhere. It was hard to believe the truth, that this world was the only one where a human had made a memory or two. The black-haired woman raised herself in the pink chair and tucked her feet beneath her, the whole of her tiny body fitting verbatim on the seat. I thought how light her skeleton must be, ready for flight. She palmed her black hair out of her face so she could get a better look, moths fluttering out of the hair, settling back into it. "You're tall," she said. "You're three times my size," she said. "Your shadow covers me completely. You look like you could be dangerous," she said, "to others maybe, but not to me. Did I ever show you my knife? It has a babyfoot charm dangling from the handle and it's clever and sharp like the sun. Your hands are large across the palm. You have shoulders close-set to your ears and this speaks of a certain power, same as how the arms are too long, really, hanging nearly to the knee, the kind of body where I'd like to watch you kill something. Or I'd like to watch you while you lift heavy objects. Or I'd like to watch you sinking slowly beneath the water."

—

She said: "Your eyes ride very far apart, like a fish or a horse. Like a fish or a horse, and so as not to startle you, I will approach you only from one side."

She said, "You sometimes look like you're sleeping when you aren't. And sometimes when you *are* sleeping you appear to be awake, eyes open. Your eyes are not the same color as my eyes. Your eyes are not the mirror of your soul. Your soul itself may be a mirror. Don't think I haven't thought of that. And how, other than the short hair of your head and the hair of your eyebrows and lashes," she said, "there's no hair on your body. Your chest looks strong but a little concave. I would like to watch you kill something and then lift it."

—

While I wondered what the word "concave" might mean, a moth climbed forth from the stack of her black hair, just over her eyes like an extra eye, as if to help the black-haired woman describe me better. It was a moth larger than the other moths, a boss moth, peeping out with its feelers, flying from her hair now toward me and landing, like a pink bow, on the head of my cock.

—

With the moth's help the black-haired woman said, "Your genitalia is mid-sized." She looked between my legs, at the moth there, at me. "It has a moth on it. The shaft seems carved out of a single piece of white branch, almost headless. Your heart beats in it a half a second after your heart beats. It doesn't have ideas of its own."

—

The pink moth flew off toward the moon and the black-haired woman followed it with her eyes.

"Watch," she said, and when she said "watch," a white bat V-ed down from the moon at the boss moth our eyes now followed, a little pop at the intersection, a cloud of pink moth-dust in the balcony light, the bat twisting off toward the moon with one half of a moth in its mouth and the other half of the moth dropping down into the wake of the houseboat *Veronica*, a torn flag for a fish.

"Do I have a name?" I asked the black-haired woman.

She looked at me. She seemed to consider my face.

"It's not clear yet," she said.

A QUICK DREAM OF THE BLACK-HAIRED WOMAN'S BLACK HAIR

—

A dream of the black-haired woman's black hair:

In the dream, I reach out to snatch the hair from her head, thinking that its splendor could only be a wig, wanting to take the wig with me where I can finally be alone with it, talk to this wig in the way it should be talked to, stroke it. So I snatch the wig from the black-haired woman's head. The hair comes off in my hand, revealing the black-haired woman's true head of hair beneath. The black-haired woman's true head of hair, beneath the wig that I've snatched, is a head of hair that appears to be an exact replica of the hair that is now in my hand, except only blacker, denser. Now, desperate, I snatch this second head of hair from her head, and beneath the second head of hair is the woman's true head of hair, again, now a third head of hair, even blacker, denser.

BUT ONCE THERE
HAD BEEN TWO OF YOU

—

Sometimes when I thought of the word "moon," I wanted to add extra Os to the word.

Sometimes when I thought of my cock I thought of a spear sticking out from the middle of my chest.

—

The black-haired woman had always lived on the houseboat *Veronica*, before me, before the counting of Time, even if she did have a belly button, which belly button seemed a keyhole. You could kneel down to that belly button. You could see a different world.

"Tell me what you see," said the black-haired woman. Then she'd let me look into this keyhole, into this other world. And then she'd let her black hair fall around me, a tent.

—

One night the black-haired woman said: "Do you remember anyone else?"

"Anyone else who?" I asked.

She waited a couple of seconds.

"Anyone else on the houseboat *Veronica?*" she asked.

I thought a little bit.

"Oh yes," I said. "Yes, I almost forgot."

—

She said, "When I put my money in your father's hand, he handed me not one boy, but two."

"Two boys," I said, nodding my head. This very well could make sense to me now. I hadn't always been the only boy on the houseboat *Veronica.*

For a short time there had been two, two boys in pink shorts, two other eyes that looked much like my eyes.

This was before the keyhole of the belly button. This was before I ever had the word "balcony" in my mouth.

—

Whoever this other boy was, in the belly hold of the houseboat *Veronica* we slept together as brothers, side by side, in matching pink shorts, this I remember. I'm not sure we were brothers, if that's how it was. I'd have to see some paperwork, take a quick look at a dictionary. We had to sleep close in the small bed of the belly hold, pressing our chests together, listening to the chuckle of the engines of the houseboat *Veronica* as it ran South or North or North or South up and down Crescent Lake, for Crescent Lake was the name of the lake, the shape of the lake.

There may have been other lakes, out in the world, if there was a world. There were certainly other boys.

There may have even been other black-haired women, but I doubted it.

—

"Witch-Surprise," this boy, my bedmate, said out loud one night.

"She'll definitely murder us if she hears you calling her names like
that," I said.

The boy blew through his lips. "I don't care about the book of bad
names. I name people how I want," he said. He said, "The black-
haired woman is a witch. There are too many teeth in her mouth. I
don't like her very much."

—

In the belly hold there was the small bed we lay in, this remembered
boy and I, and also a shower stall, a sink, a freestanding toilet flushing
straight into the lake.

On the ceiling over the small bed: a poster of the black-haired
woman, a poster of her a little bit younger, looking down at us, her
hair somehow a little bit blacker, her dress the same exact green,
same heartbreak cut.

Across from the bed: a table for the taking of breakfast and dinner,
small low table with two pink pillows for chairs.

And in one corner of the hold, near the ladderway hatch, there
stood a small black booth, with a black door, the masturbation
booth, well-constructed by the black-haired woman, where the
boy could go or I could go, into the booth alone, in case we needed
privacy when the urge came along to touch ourselves, alone I say,
and not to touch each other.

—

When I was done with myself I shut the door of the masturbation booth behind me and I crossed the belly hold and returned to the bed I shared with the boy who looked like me and smelled like me.

"The pornography in that booth is not pornography I'd choose for myself," he said. We were many arms and legs in the bed, as usual. He said, "It's all pictures of boys in pink shorts having sex with purses. It's all witches in fine deck chairs watching boys floating around underwater and playing dead. But that's not what I see in my mind at all. When I dream dreams at night I dream of real women with faces on both sides of their heads, front and back. They fly to me on rugs made of gold thread. Their feet are so soft that they squeak."

—

I myself didn't mind the pornography of the masturbation booth, found it symbolic, complex, energizing.

"The black-haired woman is always drunk and her teeth are spiny and too plentiful," the boy next to me continued.

"I wish you didn't talk that way," I said. Though I had to admit I found the teeth of the black-haired woman confusing. Small and spined, they crowded the door of her mouth, pointy-headed children trying to get out of a room all at once.

"Count your teeth with your tongue," the boy said.

I counted. "Twenty-eight," I said.

"That's the same number I get," the boy who looked like me said.

"Have you counted the black-haired woman's teeth?" I asked.

"I try," the boy had said. He said it in a voice that sounded a lot like my voice. I remember we often got confused, when talking to each other, this boy and I, as to which one of us was talking, whose turn it was to talk next.

"And?" I said.

"Was it you who just said 'and'?" he said.

"Yes," I said. "And?"

"And I always come up with a different number of teeth," he said. "The number of teeth in her mouth varies. It is always more than forty. It has never been more than sixty-three."

—

Often we could hear the footsteps of the black-haired woman above us, walking the galley of the enclosed main deck. We could hear galley drawers opening, closing. I loved those nights, calm nights, windless ones, the thrum of the engines, the smell of gasoline like a headache you were about to have. We could hear the dry snap of a match up there, the leather and pine smell of the black-haired woman's living cigarettes seeping down through the floorboards. We could hear the black-haired woman turn on the cockpit radio to listen to the weather report, small-craft warning in Sisterfield Bay, boy-raffle at the Hanging Gardens, the request of a love song, new crop of prostitutes in Torsion Cove, boy ones, girl ones, moon ones, sun ones.

"I know some things," the boy next to me said on such a night. He turned and held me close to himself. I tried to push away, for I was listening to the black-haired woman as she listened to her radio, but the boy held me tight, began listing off all the things he knew, which were not any of the things I wanted to hear. "I know I don't like working on the houseboat *Veronica*. I don't like oiling tomatoes in the garden of the balcony deck," he said. "I don't like harvesting tomatoes. I don't like sleeping here in the belly hold. I'd like to sleep beneath a star. I'd like to have the stars all over me. I don't like it that we never set foot on land. I don't like not knowing why we're here or where we came from," he said. "I think there is a world out there which is not a boat and not a lake. I think that between her legs the black-haired woman is just like you and me, the same as you and I, save the witch-talk and sex logic. I don't like her heartbreak-cut green dress. I don't like it that she's alive."

CRESCENT LAKE

—

I remembered, then and now, how I didn't like this boy. What was between the black-haired woman's legs was the business of herself and Time. What was the business of Time was the black-haired woman. So one night I left the boy there sleeping in the belly hold, alone, dreaming of his two-faced women, the ones with squeaky feet.

I did not want such women to begin polluting my dreams.

I went up the ladderway, quietly, to the galley.

I would go and see the black-haired woman about it.

—

To the side-wall of the cockpit of the houseboat *Veronica* (to the right of the captain's head if the captain were sitting at the helm) the black-haired woman (who was, herself, the captain) had taped a series of pornographic images of young men having sex with ladies' purses, purses of different style and variety, and she had also taped a navigational map of Crescent Lake, the lake upon which rode endlessly the houseboat *Veronica*.

You could look at this pornography, you could look at this map. You could learn a lot about the world you'd been living in all this time.

Good to its name the large lake, according to the map, was shaped like a crescent moon, running North and South, its two horns pointing toward the East. A river called the Little Boy River fed the northern horn of Crescent Lake at a city called Port Sisterfield. Put down your purse (if you are able) and begin your journey here, the map on the wall to your right, begin now heading gently Southwest out of Port Sisterfield, leaving the butterfly-light of that city behind, the pink lighthouses of Sisterfield Bay casting their spotlights out ahead into the darkness, you in your vessel sure and true now curling South around down-lake into an ever-fattening width until both shores of the lake could no longer be seen, not to the left nor to the right, passing the red freshwater coral of the Knee Keys, a day's easy travel over the deepest parts of the lake, rock cliffs running straight down from the sky to the bottom, the weather fine, the water clear enough you could see fat trout calibrated on their fins two hundred feet down, huge fish down there like suspended rockets, vending boats square and robotic and running by autopilot, the white- and-red-crossed bloodboats for the donating and the procuring of blood for those on the lake humanitarian of mind and/or mortally wounded, the garbage scows which need no description, the gunboats which were not boats outfitted with cannons but boats upon the decks of which you could buy small arms, Governor's Island now off the port side with its pink sand beaches, Governor's Island upon which lived no governor because there didn't seem to be any government in the time of one moon and one sun and one sky, whatever government was or could be, until you then reached, still going, still running, through the middle-most and thickest part of the lake, the voluntary prisons of the Penal Archipelago, a spray of a dozen bald islands upon which had been built towers of such geometric unattractiveness their only function could be to house imprisoned men, men imprisoned even though there seemed to be no government to imprison them, men who imprisoned themselves voluntarily for metaphysical crimes of which they had found themselves guilty, both in the future and in the past, the journey halfway over with the smell of bird shit and unwashed criminals, on South over the Formica Flats, passing heavy-bodied gasboats, trawlers of freshwater shrimp, passing knife-sailed trout boats, shaggy-looking family junk boats, spousal eyes of the sons and daughters looking over the water at nothing but you, passing fewer and fewer boats now, the lake shallowing and the shore flatter and woodsy, what small hills there were in the distance spiked with pine, the abandoned soap mine up on its ledge, little bays hungover with jillwood so that they looked like tunnels, spiked points like witch's fingers curling out into the lake, the huge Sentient Weedbeds, of orange and purple troutweed (which was in fact a single living organism twenty miles long and whispering quietly to itself), over the mudflats where the turquoise shrimp flicked, the water growing grainy and packed with baitfish and roach and turtle, the southern horn of Crescent Lake more slender and tapered than the northern, almost there, curling back East now with mosquitoes lighting in your hair, until you reached the mouth of Little Girl River and the small settlement of Torsion Cove, the dry market and the wet tavern and the brothel called the Oligarchy, feature to the lonely sailor's eye, the Oligarchy, the sagging of its walk-around porch like an exhausted lower lip, the red-lit windows of the upstairs sex-rooms, the sound of a piano like an overturned kitchen drawer coming from within.

—

And there were still other maps of Crescent Lake, these maps tacked up to the walls of the galley of the houseboat *Veronica*, like wallpaper, dozens of them. Most of the maps were expired and some maintained the familiar place names, but on some maps things had changed a lot. Though I didn't know for sure if these were maps of the lake's past or of its future, maps of parallel dimension. One map named present-day Port Sisterfield by the name Port Blossom, one map called Torsion Cove instead the Exhibition Narrows. In one map on light blue paper, even, the two towns had been reversed, Port Sisterfield in the South and Torsion Cove in the North, or rather, it was perhaps that the map had simply been flipped, as if there had been a time when the location of the poles of the earth had come under debate. On one mouse-nibbled map, likewise, the horns of Crescent Lake pointed not to the East, as the present-day map suggested, but to the West, and what I knew as the Knee Keys and the Sentient Weedbeds and the Penal Archipelago had been called instead Scarlet Woman Reef, Weedbed of the Dead, and Flying Saucer Islands. Some of these maps were unofficial maps drawn freehand on cocktail napkins and pieces of scrap paper, as if by an angler or a slaver in a bar. Some of them were maps on cured human skin (or so the black-haired woman told me) and these were maps not of the entirety of the lake but of a small special bay or a stretch of interesting and secret shore. One map—above the galley sink— spoke of a time when fishing lodges and vacation areas spotted the lake, a campground here and there, a parking lot, Xs calling out the many bait shops and taverns. Another map was a map of sex trade and noted the names and locations of prostitutes who had died in another century, sun ones and moon ones, *Cotton Annie for a good time, Tony Pillars will leave you breathless.* Another map, this one on black carbon paper, featured no place names at all, from a time when there was no language, maybe, and human beings did not swim and did not boat, a time when the human had risen too recently from the murk to think of returning to it for fun. Another map depicted the lake not as a lake but as a constellation, floating in space, the approach from Andromeda. Another map, pamphlet sized, listed the lake's haunted spots, a great plague of ghosts in that era, touting in addition to its ghosts some of the many other locations—near the old abandoned soap mine, for example, or near a children's cemetery atop a hill called Birthmark Hill—where people had been murdered memorably, murdered alone or massacred in groups. Another map listed local genocides throughout history. (There had been many genocides.) There were yet other maps. One seemed a pirate map of sites where treasure had been buried. One called Crescent Lake not Crescent Lake but Halbmond See and the language of this map was a language I could not read. One map was a map displaying the locations of lake battles fought during a conflict called the Trawler Wars, and through all maps and places, through all versions of time, back and forth from North to South and South to North, the houseboat *Veronica* sailed on endlessly, endlessly because the captain of the houseboat *Veronica*, her hair like a flock of black birds come together in a tree and her many teeth queuing forward in her mouth, never set foot on land.

A BETRAYAL

—

Three levels to the houseboat *Veronica*, bottom to top: the belly hold where I slept with the boy who looked like me and smelled like me; the enclosed main level with its galley and small bathroom and the black-haired woman's sleeping quarters; and finally the open balcony level, accessible by mercury-silver ladderways on both the fore and the aft decks.

—

I climbed from the belly hold to the galley, away from the boy who looked like me, toward the lemon and licorice smell of the black-haired woman's body. I stood in the galley, hearing the metal sleep of the solar refrigerator, the pink teapot on the stove still steaming from its snout. I turned aft and walked the narrow hallway that led to the black-haired woman's sleeping quarters, passing the small bathroom on my left. It was weird to me, who didn't know of math or physics, how a boat could be going one direction, and I, on that boat (in that boat?), could walk, without trouble, somehow in the opposite direction. It shouldn't have worked. But it always did.

—

I didn't find the black-haired woman in her sleeping quarters. I walked the lush green of its carpeting to the sliding aft doors and

I stepped out onto the aft deck, its two umbrellaed fishing chairs near the aft rail and the black and wooden cleaning table, dully spangled with fish scales.

The black-haired woman was not there, on the aft deck, either.

But now I could hear her up on the balcony level, with the night, talking to herself as the boat chugged along, talking to herself, maybe, of sun ones, moon ones, a storm coming in. She seemed to me a lonely kind of person in some ways. Over the aft rail the surface of Crescent Lake appeared a pretty lacquered white. I could see one shore of Crescent Lake but not the other. I thought I could see the twinkle of the southern toe of Governor's Island, still miles away from the voluntary prisons of the Penal Archipelago, where men sentenced themselves to wait and die. I could smell the spice and rot of the forest coming in on the wind. I could hear mosquitoes on the near shoreline, those many little things humming like one large thing.

"Hello," I said up the ladderway.

"Who goes there?" said the black-haired woman.

"It's me," I said.

"Can you be more specific?" she asked.

I thought about it.

"No," I said.

—

The mercury railing, the light poles, the smell of the black-haired woman's body even in that open space.

I'd come up there to tell the black-haired woman that a boy who looked a lot like me (but who most certainly was *not* me) really wanted her dead. It felt like a dangerous thing to be doing and I advised myself a certain care. The black-haired woman stood at the rail, facing that closest shore, bottle of yellow benzene in one hand, the shore sliding by, the moon above her like an idea, one small white hand on the mercury rail, her black hair like a rip in time where space was leaking out (or vice versa).

"I'm very glad you're here," the black-haired woman said. She looked up at the sky. "I'm not sure where the moon has gotten to."

"It's above your head," I said, pointing. "You can't see it because of your hair."

She looked, tilting herself far back, hands woozily on her hips, and there she saw the moon.

"Tricky thing," she said to it.

—

She stepped from the rail and palmed back her hair. In the balcony garden the tomatoes shone like little overheated faces in the vines. The black-haired woman walked on tiptoe to the balcony table, her toe-points tapping like hooves on the brazierwood decking. You could see, now that she tiptoed, how she had that pink-handled knife in her hand, the dangling of the babyfoot charm, the knife brought from her heartbreak-cut green dress just in case mine was not a friendly moonlight visit, I supposed, and I meant to be her killer. I worried she saw her killers everywhere. I worried she imagined that I had all these ideas I did not have. Death was all around me in those days, even in me, maybe. It was surprising how rarely I cared. I saw how big my shadow was, a monster's shadow, compared to her small body. I sat down on the deck to make this shadow smaller. She sat at the table, crossed her legs like a boy, her long-toed feet looking somewhat like hands. With the benzene in her she moved carefully, her eyes fixed on the middle distance, like she listened to a voice no one else could hear, a voice that told her how to do it all, how to be a witch, step by simple step. I wondered if she knew how highly I regarded her. I wanted to compliment the pornography she left for us in the masturbation booth, to thank her for having built the booth to begin with (very thoughtful!) and to thank her for the pink shorts I wore. There was a bruise on her left shin, shape of a heart cut in half.

She said, "The thing about the sun, there's no missing it. The moon, though, you can't always say where it'll be. I suppose there were people," she said, "who knew where to look when they looked for the moon, who could point it out blindfolded and be right." She upended the bottle. Talking like this seemed to make her happy. "Another thing is," she said, wiping her mouth with the back of her hand, "is how the sun is always there, during the day. It almost never fails. But the moon, at night, sometimes it isn't there at all. And then," she said, "sometimes you'll even see the moon during the day, up there where it isn't supposed to be, even when the sun is out." She shook her head. What she spoke of seemed a wonder to her. "And when the moon comes out during the day," she said, "I often have bad dreams. It's seeing the moon when it's daylight," she said, thinking, counting on one finger, looking at me now, "and it's whenever I see blood."

"What's whenever you see blood?"

"When I see the moon during the day, or, then, when I see blood before I go to sleep," she said. "On those occasions I have weird dreams. My blood, someone else's blood."

She passed the bottle of benzene to me. I looked at the bottle, little twigs and silt, took a drink, tasted sulfur and the cemetery, a volcano on the moon.

"Would you ever tell me about a dream you've had?" I asked.

I was curious what a witch might dream about. I imagined pet locusts. I imagined demon husbands.

"Maybe when we're better friends," she said, looking off.

I worried I'd made some mistake. I redirected. "I never thought to check about seeing my own blood," I said, "and then having a bad dream afterward."

I handed the bottle back to her.

"It happens," she said. "You should keep it in mind."

"Next time I bleed?"

"Next time you bleed," she said.

—

We sat looking at each other, or at least I sat looking at her. It worried me how much taller I was. Even sitting I seemed massive in comparison. The benzene opened up a little box in my chest and inside that box there was a smaller box and I climbed inside, got small. I could have named all the invisible hairs on her knees. Her black eyes stayed difficult to see in the rough of her giant black hair. You didn't always know what she might be looking at. A pink moth dripped from the curl of hair over her eyes and she lit a match off the rough underside of her left heel, brought it to the broad tip of one of the living pink cigarettes she always had at the ready. The moth flew to me and landed on my chest.

The cigarette looked huge, like a pink dessert, in the black-haired woman's small hand.

"You have something to say," she said.

I nodded. I brushed the moth away. "You're aware that there's another boy on this boat, a boy who looks like me, who also wears pink shorts?"

"I'm aware," she said.

"Tonight," I'd said, getting to it, "this boy—not me, I'm saying, but the *other* boy—he said some things about you."

Smoke leaked from between her teeth, which were spiny and, at present, teeming, too many for me to count. Not that I was counting. She asked, "What exactly did the other boy say?"

—

Standing at the railing now, her back to me, she pulled her dress high and held the hem between her chin and chest while she pissed hands-free through the mercury-silver railing, down the two stories to the lake. I felt a certain ache in my chest to see this privacy. The high arc of the stream reminded me of the double rainbow-like arches of her feet. I looked away. Looking away I told her what the boy who looked like me and smelled like me had said about her, that he had called her "Witch-Surprise," that he didn't like it how she was alive. She sat down at the table again, slowly, carefully, listening to the inner voice, I guessed, that told her what it was, next, to be a witch, what might be made to die and who might be allowed to live. She let her eyes roll back in her head and, with her thought, the houseboat *Veronica* picked up speed. And she asked me then, directly, if I planned to murder her. I said to her how I didn't plan to, no. She told me sometimes murder happened without a plan. She said how sometimes people got confused about the feelings they were feeling. I asked her if it was possible, in that case, to have on hand a plan to *not* murder someone, no matter under what conditions, not even a spur of the moment kind of thing. Or, I asked her, maybe it would be possible, in order that I not get confused about the feelings I was feeling, that I could be *told* what feelings I was feeling, or at least have these feelings explained to me. She admitted this might be possible but she'd have to think on it a while.

She thought on it a while. Then she looked over and she said, "You're feeling like you trust me very much."

I checked with the feelings I was feeling and I said, "I'm feeling like I trust you very much."

She said, "You're feeling very calm and like you might want to have me describe you again."

I said, standing up and taking off the pink shorts, "I'm feeling very calm and very much like I might want to have you describe me again."

She said, "I think I would like that," and I stood before her and she described my body to me again, pointing out some asymmetry to the hips, pointing out what she thought might have been a flaw in the collarbone, perhaps broken before I was making memories, back in the time before the black-haired woman's money had entered my father's hand. And she spoke to me that way late into the night, about murder, about long lakes and small boats, about my body and other serious things. And I became aware, close to dawn, during the black-haired woman's slurring talk, that I could hear the voices of men singing, off in the distance. Clearly the boat now approached the voluntary prisons of the Penal Archipelago. I'd heard this singing before, in the life I'd come down with, after the black-haired woman's money had loosed my body from my father's hand, down in the belly hold of the houseboat *Veronica*, the prisoners there in the towers, singing in the night to each other. I was always remembering things I hadn't remembered before. This remembering was often danger-ous to one's innocence. I could see the stand-alone towers of the voluntary prisons, tall and thin, lit with roving spotlights of a green that matched the black-haired woman's heartbreak-cut green dress. There were a dozen or so islands, to each island a tower.

"At night I like to sit and listen to the men singing," she said. "Did I tell you," she said, "that my son is a prisoner there?" With a finger-like thumb she pointed, over her shoulder, behind her, toward the islands of the Penal Archipelago.

"I didn't know you had a son," I said. At the word "son" I felt a hook of feeling in my stomach, both when she said it and when I said it, "son." She nodded and closed her black eyes, which made them look white.

"The sound of their voices makes me feel very strong," she said. "Strong and somehow sleepy. Men who have sentenced themselves to wait and die. This is quite a world. Life stops being an important thing," she said, "but death never does, thank goodness, which is two ways of saying the same thing, I guess. What I do is I close my eyes and listen to the voices of the men singing. I try to single out my son's voice. I'm not sure if he sings at all, with rest of the men, when the houseboat *Veronica* approaches. Or if he's being stub-born. Or if he's a man by now. Or if I even remember his voice. I have a lot of fans in that prison, many admirers. I hope my son is one of them. I hope his voice is a beautiful voice." She blew the last of the smoke of her pink cigarette down toward me, where I sat at her feet. I breathed the smoke in (on purpose) and with it came the feeling of little tails twitching in my veins.

"Why did your son go to prison?"

"He checked himself in for his terrible crimes."

"What terrible crimes?" I asked.

She stubbed the cigarette on the heel of her foot.

"He was in love with me," she said.

IT WAS A LITTLE SAD WHEN
IT FINALLY HAPPENED

—

Closer to dawn the black-haired woman nodded off (or pretended to) and I left her to her peace, went down the ladderway to the aft deck, through the black-haired woman's sleeping quarters, into the galley again and returned down the ladderway to the belly hold.

"Some people in pink shorts," the boy who looked like me said from the bed we shared, "are trying to fucking sleep."

I didn't care for the obscenity. I lay down next to this boy. He rolled to turn away. At this point in my life I had not murdered anyone, but I could feel the possibility in me, a coin loose in a purse. I looked at the back of the boy's head. I tried to look through his skull and out from his eyes. I knew it likely that the black-haired woman, now knowing her assassination was a topic belowdecks, might murder indiscriminately, murder me, or murder the other boy and murder both of us, murder both of us and just start over with new boys, murder us both before I or the other boy could murder her, not that I was going to murder her, I just mean how it might have added up in the black-haired woman's mind. I didn't want to die. At this point on the houseboat *Veronica*, as I may have said, I was not yet a bride. I'd yet to be involved in the fashion of the black-haired woman's lovemaking. I admit I was a boy curious what marriage might be, thought very much about her long toes, what her body might look like without the business of its clothes and her mind belonging half to Time. I looked at the muscled back of the sleeping boy next to me and I imagined plunging a knife (a knife I did not have) into the strength of that back. The boy rolled over just as I stabbed him in my secret mind and he threw one arm around me. Out of his half-sleep he said the sentence, "Bells are ringing."

I poked him in the ribs and I told him a lie. "You better get up there. She wants to talk to you."

—

What kind of son could the black-haired woman have had? Would this baby have been delivered by way of her belly or her hand or through the pupil of the left eye? And what kind of son would not sing to a mother from his high prison at night when she came by in her amazing thought-controlled boat to hear him? Alone in the small bed of the belly hold, I listened as closely as I could to the singing of the men in the voluntary prisons of the Penal Archipelago. I thought of the half-heart-shaped bruise on the black-haired woman's shin and I stood up from bed and walked to the masturbation booth and closed myself inside so I could better touch myself and think about the black-haired woman. Just beneath the sound of the men singing from the towers of the voluntary prison, I could hear the black-haired woman's voice: up on the balcony deck she was talking, I knew, to the boy who looked like me and smelled like me. I could hear his voice too, a voice that sounded a lot like mine, but insolent, stalling, brave. It was my doing that he was up there. I felt sad, but not enough to stop it. I doubted I could have stopped it anyway. I knelt in the booth and I thought of the black-haired woman's belly button, the fingerlike stretch of her toes. I heard the hooflike rap of the black-haired woman going up on her tiptoes and moving swiftly across the deck above me, no doubt the murder taking place in real time. In my mind I could see the flash of the black-haired woman's pink-handled knife, the babyfoot charm dangling from the handle, the horror and the grace. I heard the voice of the boy who looked like me cut off in the middle of making a noise I hadn't heard him make before, also a noise I had not heard myself make before. I heard the black-haired woman's calm voice saying something I couldn't make out, a hushing. Then quiet for a little, with the sound of men singing from the voluntary prison towers, then I heard the splash of the boy's body as it hit the surface of Crescent Lake. I imagined the black-haired woman standing over the rail, watching the boy's body sinking down, like a moth, beneath the waves. I knew this to be a significant death. Probably I was the only boy who looked like me left alive in the world.

IN WHICH YOU ARE GIVEN A NAME

—

The afternoon after the murder of the boy who had once looked like me, the black-haired woman sat on her cute-set chair on the balcony deck, beneath the black umbrella. She'd drawn greasepaint bars under her eyes to block the sun bouncing off the deck and the bars looked butch and fetching. She watched while I shined, with trout oil and rag, the tomatoes of the little balcony garden. We were now a family. And while I worked, she sang a little song for me, like a spell, her voice low and high, maybe a spell to keep me working, maybe a spell to keep me breathing, "how will you see me when the rain doesn't have eyes / how will you drown me when the fish are on my side?"

"Where did you learn such a song?" I asked her.

She said: "Last night, in a dream, you sang it to me."

"I did?"

"You sang it to me," she said. "You asked me to sing it next time I saw you."

—

"What did you say to him before you murdered him?" I asked.

"Who?" she said.

"The boy who looked like me," I said.

"How do you know I said anything?"

"I could hear a little of it," I said.

She touched a fingertip to my nose, like it was a button. She said, "I took out my knife and I said to him: 'I'm pretty sure I'm murdering the right boy.'"

———

A witch, she was there, and she wasn't, she wasn't and she was.

The day had a pelt, the night sometimes had scales. Hot nights of me, sleeping in the belly hold, in the bed without the other boy, levitating at the magnet of the black-haired woman's footfall abovedeck, uncharmable nights wishing the boy who once looked like me might return from the dead (empty of blood, full of regret) and climb back onto the houseboat *Veronica*, if only so that the black-haired woman could murder him again, murder him again and again not murder me, to have been selected like I'd been selected, to have been spared for something, the black-haired woman's spells in my hair, how she keeps me on the green side of the ledger for the future's use, my terrible masturbation in the dark of the masturbation booth, my belly full of salted tomato slices and blueing shrimp. I could smell the licorice and lemon of the black-haired woman's body everywhere, imagined her breath on my neck like a little sun. In the masturbation booth I stood, and I knelt, said things aloud, taking myself in hand, hoping for the black-haired woman to overhear me, things like "I am not truly insignificant," and "Lonely sex act performed by boy in pink shorts," and, at just the right moment, "Candle with the little wick of bone inside."

Not many people know what it's like to be spared, the heart inflated by rip cord, the heave of it coming up your throat, your own blood something you're barely able to get away with.

I said to myself, alone in the booth, "Death is a baby full of death."

It was a line that didn't seem to be my line to say, but I said it anyway.

I was getting stronger and stronger.

Not many people get to love a witch.

—

One night the black-haired woman called me to the balcony deck to watch flocks of night-birds threading themselves across the moon (she sat in my lap on the cute-set deck chair; she let me hold one of her long-toed feet in my hand like a pet while she voiced her bird names in my ear); on another night she invited me into the galley for a cup of strong tea and benzene over the batwing-bound book of bad names, which she hauled forth from beneath her huge bed, the space-volcano of the benzene in my belly, long and rambling horror stories starring her and her knife alone, a new entry now for the boy who had called her Witch-Surprise, the boy who looked like me no longer and who no longer breathed like me, babyfoot charm dangling from the pink handle of her knife, her speech slurring into other languages; another night I awoke, in my bed in the belly hold, with the black-haired woman standing over me, saying yet more strange words and making guttural shapes with her hands; and another night (the night of all nights!)

she called me up to the balcony level so I could see the memorial she'd made on the spot where she'd murdered the boy who once looked like me.

—

Sleepily I followed her up the mercury ladderway and over, the night sky dropping netlike around, the Penal Archipelago reeling along starboard. For two days and nights we'd circled the Penal Archipelago, each night anchoring off a different grouping of towers so that the black-haired woman could listen to the imprisoned men who sang out to her.

"There," she said, crossing the balcony deck. She pointed over to the starboard deck railing, the spot where the murder of the boy would've happened, the boat beneath us sighing and her hair like a black thumbprint on the moon behind her. "He stood there like you could stand if you wanted, with his back to me, like a boy would, or with your back to me, looking out over the lake." She pushed me forward. She pointed down to the memorial she'd made. I was standing on it. What it was was a circle carved by suit knife into the brazierwood decking, a couple stars for design, two footprints carved also within the circle, meant to mark the place where the boy who looked like me had stood in the universe with his back to the black-haired woman, not knowing that Time no longer considered him interesting. It was a balcony deck, but it was hallowed ground. The black-haired woman stepped close behind me, her face between my shoulder blades, hands on my hips, the pink moths of her hair fluttering around me like they wanted to make a scarf.

"Like this," the black-haired woman said, raising one hand to my throat, knife-free, drawing her hand ear to ear, showing me how it went.

—

I looked down at the charmed circle I stood within, bloodless and sweet. I looked up and saw how the stars were getting all over me.

"Orphan Thing," she said, giving me a name from amongst the names. "Orphan Thing," she said, separating me from the dead. I turned to face her. "All right," she said, and when she said "all right" a large pink moth, this one with white polka dots on its wings, eased out of the black-haired woman's hair, flung itself forth and landed on my chest, between the nipples, like an extra nipple if I should ever need one. I wondered if there were any people left alive other than the black-haired woman and Orphan Thing. I felt all my molecules meet each other, sniffing each other like dogs, the tiny pinprick as the moth flattened and began to drink my blood, at long last, now that the boy who once looked like me was dead, the white spots of the moth's wings going pink and fast with my blood. I was Orphan Thing. Pretty soon, I could tell, I was going to have to invent the word "love."

"I'd really like to hunt you," the black-haired woman said dreamily, "but so far you never try to escape."

"I won't," I said.

She said: "You're younger than me, but, because of this, I knew a much younger world. Your world started off very old and I'm sorry." She watched the moth, now heavy, lift off and gutter once about my head. She touched at the moth bite with a long white finger. She said, "Tonight you'll dream a dream where you have at least two wings. You'll dream of a day when men in strange outfits discover your blood on the moon."

A VISION

—

The moths flew out and fed from me once more and again. The black-haired woman stepped back, hands on hips, to watch it happen, the knife with its babyfoot charm in her left hand, her long toes making her taller, the knife at the ready, I guess, in case I didn't like what the moths were doing and might try to flee from her or attack. A little it wounded me that she didn't know me better. I knew I wasn't her killer. But how to prove this to her, to anyone? More moths flew from her hair, more drank from my blood. And one by one, once they'd fattened, the moths lifted off, bounced back to the coverage of the black-haired woman's hair, ferrying my blood to her. I didn't want to change. I wanted to be the perfect gift, one to be drained forever. I could feel my blood, what had been in me, now flying through the air on wings, escaping its weight, becoming part of the black-haired woman's system. I dropped to my knees on the brazierwood decking and looked at the toes of her feet.

"It's made you very sleepy," the black-haired woman said. She clapped her hands and the last of the moths lifted off my skin, at once, and flew back to her hair, like snapped into it by elastic string. She leaned her small face down over mine. She said, "It's a beautiful night. Why don't you lie down for a while?"

—

I awoke I don't know when, though still night, my blood growing
back like memories, the houseboat *Veronica* anchored in a calm bay
just off the voluntary prisons of the Penal Archipelago. Three prison
towers rose like the tines of a huge fork and the houseboat *Veronica*
knelt small before them, swaying gently in the waves. High up, each
tine speared and held aloft a saucerlike fortress, the prisons themselves, one, two, three. Small, barred windows lined each fortress-top
and greasy yellow light leaked from within, men and their faces the
size of moths up there, but their voices strong. They sang of the black-
haired woman, of the loveliness of her form, of the quickness of her
mind and knife, the sturdiness of the houseboat *Veronica*. The black-
haired woman stood at the prow end of the balcony deck with her
back to me, her hair lit by the gentle light of the four-cornered light
poles jumping up from the mercury railing. She stood at the railing,
confronting the towers, pinchbottle of benzene empty in her hand
and the tines of the towers rising from the lake before her, her arms
lifting toward the singing men. Drunk she tossed the empty bottle
toward the tower. Still weak from the moths I pushed myself up onto
my elbows to better see this vision. Some men hollered down at her
and some laughed happily to see her there, below them, on the balcony deck of the houseboat *Veronica*, that famous vessel they sang
of. There was applause and there was some whistling. The men had
access to matches or somehow fire and they tossed burning clumps
of toilet paper from the windows and these burning clumps dropped
like plunked birds from the towers. The men sang and sang on. They
sang a song of arms and legs and black hair. The black-haired woman,
her back to me still, swept her hair up in her two hands, made a stack
on top of her head, defiant, so that her neck and shoulders could be
seen. Therefore, the men then sang of necks and of shoulders. Sway-
ingly with the benzene in her blood, the black-haired woman lifted

her green heartbreak-cut dress over her head, let the dress drop in a pool at her feet. Some of the singing voices stopped singing then, as if the sight of her without the business of her clothes was too complete to add lyrics to. I saw her neck and her shoulder blades myself. I didn't want to look away. I wished that she were facing me so that I could see her complete, not just her body but also her face, her face with her hair up like that and a neck for her head, but I made no noise. You could hear one prisoner, high up in the central tower, begin weeping like someone he loved had died, weeping to see the black-haired woman without her storied dress. One man shouted out his undying love for the black-haired woman. Another man shouted out how no one knew what was in his heart. The black-haired woman stood there for some time this way, nude and facing the towers of imprisoned men, one of whom was possibly her son, or so I imagined, motionless except for the flex of her knees as the boat rolled with the waves. The black-haired woman turned at the hip and looked at me (I had not known she knew that I was watching her) and she smiled around her too many teeth. How many teeth? I hoped that she'd never die. I hoped she had exactly as many teeth as she wanted. She turned back toward the towers and stood there until all the singing men stopped singing, pink moths fluttering about her hair, white bats dipping down like wolves from the moon, though on second glance there didn't seem to be a moon anymore, at least not where it could be found, and I looked at the form of the black-haired woman, the tower light holding her body with its green, and I thought to myself how I knew a little better, now, what a mother was.

THE FOUR-HANDED WHITE FOG

—

In her sleeping quarters, the next night or the same night, I recite to her aloud a letter I've written for her. With some formal-
ity I recite a letter to her while she listens from the bed. It is
not a letter I have written, exactly, as I am a boy not supposed
to hold a pen in my hand. It's a letter I've memorized, therefore,
with my mind.

—

Dear Black-Haired Woman,

I know you don't want any written testament laying around.

Therefore, I don't use a pen and I don't know your name either.

In marriages, I have heard, one person may take the other person's
name. I'm not saying I think you would be interested in marrying.
But if you had a name you ever wanted to tell me about, I'm sure I
wouldn't mind keeping the name as my own.

I like your heartbreak-cut green dress. Your body is small, and I
worry for it. When you stand on the balcony deck, when you stand
too close to the mercury railing, I want to tie a rope around your
middle, so that you won't fall off into the water.

I worry about this during storms and rough weather. In a nightmare I see you floating off into the sky.

—

More than once you've asked me if I remember the thing called parents. I don't. But I do have this dream, and I want to tell you about it.

This is the dream of the four-handed white fog.

The four-handed white fog isn't a monster.

I'm asleep in a bed. There's a crooked tree out the window. It seems important, beyond mentioning the tree, to say that I'm on land. There is a floor beneath me and around that floor a house and beneath that house is the ground and not the water. I am all alone. I don't think I'm making it up. The four-handed white fog comes down the hall, enters my bedroom. "We're not a monster," the four-handed white fog says from the doorway.

"Come on in," I say.

"We're here about the milk," the four-handed white fog says.

"I don't know about the milk," I say.

"It was our milk," the four-handed white fog says, "and we had been looking forward to drinking it."

"I had a milk once," I say, "but I think it was a long time ago."

"When you lie," the four-handed white fog says, "it makes us worry you won't become a member of society."

"Leave me alone," I say.

"There was a milk, but there isn't a milk anymore," says the four-handed white fog. "This absence of milk needs to be addressed."

"Maybe one of you drank it and forgot," I say to the four-handed white fog.

"There is only one of us," says the four-handed white fog, "and we'd never forget the drinking of milk."

—

I'm not sure, with this dream, if I'm dreaming something real, or something made up, or something in the future. With your help I've made a secret study of the differences between the sun and the moon, and there are many complications and similarities to keep track of, but the difference between a dream and a memory is even more confusing. I close here saying only that I think your feet are handsome and by signaling my willingness to let the question of parents drop.

There are no longer two boys on the houseboat *Veronica*. I am the living one, the one who likes purses and tomatoes.

Yours Truly,

Orphan Thing

BANG-KNIVES AND OTHER KNIVES

—

The black-haired woman carried with her, always somewhere in her hair or in the pockets of her heartbreak-cut green dress, the sickle-bladed suit knife with the pink handle and the lacquered babyfoot charm dangling from it, shining like luck. I knew there to be a fillet knife sheathed on the scarred cleaning table of the aft deck. I knew there to be another fillet knife in one of the kitchen drawers of the galley. I knew the black-haired woman slept with a long stiletto slipped between the mattress and the box springs. I knew she kept a serrated hunting knife on a shower shelf in the small bathroom, in case she ever would be surprised while showering. I knew she kept hidden in the mass of her black hair a doll-house scalpel, braided down close to the nap. But there were still other knives on the houseboat *Veronica*, knives I hadn't been introduced to yet.

—

"Do you think there'll be a Winter?" I asked.

The black-haired woman ignored me.

"Have I showed you one of these before?" she asked, opening her hand. What was in her hand didn't look like a knife. Or it looked like the handle of a knife, but with no knife sticking from it, a little black bar, really. I'd never seen one before. We were sitting cross-legged on her huge bed, side by side, weather blowing in and the houseboat *Veronica* climbing and falling. She had a couple other bang-knives dropped on the mattress around her, little black lengths from a dumped cardboard case of them. "It's like a switch-blade but different," she said. She showed me the knife in her hand, closely. There was a silver button, on the length, where your thumb would go. Also, she showed me where the little cartridge went. She let the cartridge fall into her hand, held it up so I could look, slipped it back into the handle, closed the clasp. "Like this," she said. She twisted to face the headboard and lifted the bang-knife. "Three times," she said, and she pressed the silver button three times. There was a muffled pop in her hand, like a tiny gunshot, and you couldn't see the blade come out, and then the blade was just there, a blur thunking two feet free of its handle, wagging from the headboard like a tail.

"Bang-knife," I said.

"They don't make them anymore," she said.

—

The spent bang-knife smoked in her hand, a husk. She tossed it onto the green carpet.

"Face me," she said.

We faced each other on the huge white bed. She handed me one of the other bang-knives. I held it in my hand. She took my hand and lifted it so that the business end of the bang-knife rested in the hollow of her throat.

She said, "Your hand is nice and warm."

—

We sat that way a long time, the boat falling and rising, me wondering about Winter and holding the bang-knife to the black-haired woman's throat. This made me very uncomfortable as I didn't want to murder her. It seemed the wrong way around. I met what I believed were her eyes and I suppose we looked at each other for a while. After a while the black-haired woman opened her mouth and wet her finger on her tongue. You could hear the world out there, outside the boat, rolling unhurried, like it believed it might even last a little bit longer. She leaned forward and wiped the spit beneath my left eye, marking a chevron on my cheek. She opened her hand and I dropped the bang-knife into it.

"No one died," she said.

WHERE WERE YOU WHEN YOU REALIZED THERE WAS ANOTHER WORLD?

—

Notes in the black-haired woman's vibrating penmanship, notes of instruction for boat work, or when I should go for a swim to clean my body, or when to polish the mercury railing, unslat the brazierwood decking, letting the slats stand in the health of moonlight, a lot of work stacking up without the other boy around anymore, or weeding the balcony-level garden, plucking it free of insects and worms, or to shave my head, which was the only hair of my body which grew. Sometimes the black-haired woman's notes asked me to take the throw nets from their aft storage cabinet and stay on the lookout, throughout the day, for schools of baitfish. Some days were called laundry days, and with smooth lake stones I'd pound the black-haired woman's green heartbreak-cut dresses, for there were more than just one dress in all her closets, an unending number, which crop of green dresses I'd hang carefully to dry while the black-haired woman drank and supervised. Sometimes the notes in her handwriting reminded me how my name was Orphan Thing. Sometimes the notes reminded *her* that my name was Orphan Thing, as every now and then—even though she'd named me—she did manage to forget my name. Sometimes the notes reminded me that once, on the houseboat *Veronica*, there had been another boy, one who looked like me but no longer breathed like me, this language next to a nice little drawing of a sad-faced skeleton.

—

What I liked most about these notes, though, was the black-haired woman's handwriting itself. It seemed to vibrate up and off the paper, a constellation hovering. I liked coming up the ladder from the belly hold to see her penmanship rising from whatever note she'd left for me on the galley table, her penmanship an even more sacred system than the dresses of her body. To the eye the penmanship looked spidery and light, each letter leaning back on the letter prior, as if the letters in the words and sentences she wrote were trying hard not to fall over a cliff or wanted to spend more time with each other before they lifted off to deliver their information. The handwriting looked light, yes, but you could feel the dents in the paper, the grooves the pencil or the pen made in the power of her hand, the force of her hand behind what she wanted to say. One of the best things was, even prior to having read such a note, to lay my palm on the surface, in order to feel the whorls and dents of the black-haired woman's code. It felt, beneath your hand, her handwriting, like the bark of a tree, like running your hand over the surface of a dry lakebed.

—

Sometimes I'd take this penmanship with me down into the hold and sneak it into the masturbation booth, so I could take my time. Her handwriting, I believed, was part of the fashion of her love-making, an early signpost: whenever I saw the way her *e*'s leaned back on her *s*'s I felt my mouth water and the blood run away from my head. Every time she wrote my name, Orphan Thing, it located me to the stars and how their heat could be felt, in my eyes and on my skin, even from that distance. The other boy, when he had been alive, had not liked any of this kind of thing, not the sex of the black-haired woman's penmanship, not the boat work in general, not the way you would sometimes catch the black-haired woman overseeing you from the balcony deck while you mopped the brazierwood foredecking, her black eyes cool upon your body, like shade.

A VISITOR

—

A different day among the many days, the sun like a little magnifying glass.

"How will you pay?" the white-bearded man said, his voice with a little rattle in it, like it was a voice he, this man, was somehow still getting used to. The man was a human man and he was alive. The beard he wore was a false beard, for the wisdom and masculinity of it. He spoke over water from the deck of the gasboat, there in the lake just a boat-length off the aft deck of the houseboat *Veronica*. Gas fumes pulsed off him as he watched the black-haired woman cleaning fish, then he let his eyes touch over at me, beside her, there where I sat on the aft railing. We lay anchored again, for refueling, a mile or so from the Penal Archipelago. It was easy enough, in this world, to say "mile." You could look off starboard and see the prison towers geometric, like ugly flowers, in the sun. The white-bearded man was the only person we'd seen, on the lake, in some number of days. He slotted the gas pump into its holster and looked up from behind the console of the gasboat at the black-haired woman, to see if she'd answer him. She stood on tiptoes, behind the scarred cleaning table, the fillet knife in her hand.

"Your beard is ridiculous," she said to him.

"Never mind the beard," he said.

"Trade then," she said, keeping both levels of her voice empty. "I've got shrimp and tomatoes. I've got bait and cherries. There are some books around no one's reading. I've got some trinkets. Some things in cans."

"I'm not too good around books," the white-bearded gasman said. He kept fiddling with the elastic that kept the beard tight behind his ears. The gasboat drifted closer to the *Veronica* and he reached out with a butting pole to push himself away from us, but the butting pole would not quite touch the side of the *Veronica* yet, so he just stood there with the pole stuck out in front of him. His eyes measured what of worth could be seen on our decks, his mouth lurking vulnerable behind his false beard.

"How about the boy?" he said.

"How about him what?" the black-haired woman said. She palmed the heat of her hair from her face.

"Just an hour's say," the white-bearded man said.

The black-haired woman looked at me.

"There isn't any hour," she said.

"Fifteen minutes," the white-bearded man said.

"Nor any minutes either," she said.

The white-bearded man looked around him, looked at the cracked console, looked down at his feet. "It does get lonely on this boat," he said.

"Sorry about that," the black-haired woman said.

"Look I didn't mean anything by it," the white-bearded man said.

"What would you mean if you'd meant something by it?" she asked.

"I'm just saying," the white-bearded man said, "don't pay me any mind."

"I won't pay you any mind," the black-haired woman said. She flicked the fillet knife so that it stuck standing up, like a bit of punctuation, from the cleaning table.

"I can see you don't care if a person is lonely or not," the white-bearded man said.

AN ESCAPED PRISONER

—

A little while later, the white-bearded gasman paid and gone, the black-haired woman said to me, "I've got an idea about you." She winked broadly and dipped her hand into the live well, held up a living catfish in her hand, stepped back to the cleaning table. She took up the pliers, clamped the underside of the fish's jaw. With her fillet knife she made a shallow cut around the plated skull, all around the bone to the soft of the throat and through the throat, the tail of the fish curling toward the black-haired woman's knife hand, as if it would touch her one last time. She hummed at this work and she rested the knife on the cleaning board, dished the pliers to her left, held the head of the fish down with her right, careful of the pectoral spines. With her thumb she worried the skin from the flesh, working it looser, clamping the pliers onto the flap of skin she'd made. She pulled and peeled the fish whole from its skin, cutting off the head, unfastening the laundry of the guts. She found the small heart with the tip of her knife and she fed it to herself. You could see the heart impaled on the spine of her eyetooth, still pumping. She flipped the guts over the railing and into the water, where a gull floated in close, making its catlike noises.

"What's your idea about me?" I asked.

She dropped the cleaned fish into the live well at her feet and looked over at me.

"What?" she said.

"You said you had an idea about me," I said.

She looked out over the lake.

"I totally forgot what I was going to say," she said.

—

"I like your penmanship," I said to her.

She nodded, passed over what I'd said, as I'd said it many times before. She rinsed her small hands in the live well and sat down next to me on the aft deck, her candle-thin legs half the length of mine. "I like an afternoon like this," she said, leaning her head on my shoulder, the heat of her great hair, like a fire burned in the core of it, her words coming slowly, like she listened to a voice that told her what words were the ones to say, how to feel them in her mouth, "an afternoon that still has a little bit of morning in it, and you can hear the wind and the waves, and it's hard to tell one from the other, and you don't know and don't care if there's going to be a Winter, and you've forgotten half the spells you've ever sent out into this world, and you're on the aft deck of your own true boat, and you're hanging out with Orphan Thing, and there's a lot of room on the boat because there isn't anyone else on the boat anymore, and all that room and all that sunlight makes you feel like getting married."

—

Toward evening we lay off the Penal Archipelago while the black-haired woman fished for trout just over the rock bottom. She caught no trout. She shaved my head with the pink-handled knife she'd murdered the other boy with, its babyfoot charm dangling down in my face. She told me how my hair didn't have a part at all, just spirals and conflagrations. This made me feel proud for some reason. I fell asleep with her hands tilting my head this way and that. She woke me and asked me to stand so she could describe me. She described me and then we stood together and looked over the aft railing toward the Penal Archipelago.

—

"Look out there," she said, pointing out at the lake. I looked to where she was looking, where she was pointing. "An escaped prisoner," she said.

Now I saw what she saw, a small dark head struggling through the waves toward the houseboat *Veronica*. A swimmer coming our way. The black-haired woman shaded her eyes and stood balanced on the railing to get a better look. I steadied her with my hands on her hips, so narrow I could touch my fingertips together, her small collection of molecules.

"It's my son," the black-haired woman said.

—

In the end, I suppose, there wasn't much to it. I wasn't sure any of it was real. It was like I was seeing into her head, the way the world arrived through her eye, blundering away with a vision I wouldn't have been able to have otherwise. From the protected waters of the archipelago a guard boat turned sluggishly, pointed its snub nose in the direction of the escaped swimmer, who was also the black-haired woman's son, a voice like an angry robot coming distantly from the boat's megaphones. You could sentence yourself to the voluntary prison, but the guard boat said how you couldn't just unsentence yourself. That would be ridiculous. There were going to have to be consequences. Consequences were what made things real. We watched the guard boat, orange and ugly, a siren like a red berry on top. The black-haired woman sat now on the aft railing with her candle legs dangling over, so as to better watch her son attempt to reach her, the smell of benzene coming sweet from her armpits. We could make out the voice of the megaphone now, asking the swimmer to turn back, we could see men on the deck of the guard boat, holding onto the railing against the speed of the boat, long black spears in their hands, sticking up stiff like eyelashes from the deck. The guard boat cut its engines. The prisoner, treading water now, twirled in the water to face down the boat. A guard holding a long black spear with a barbed silver tip walked out onto the catwalk of the guard boat. Three or so other guards braced on the deck, waving, looking over the rail, shouting instructions up to the cockpit. The guard with the black spear leaned over the railing of the catwalk and pointed the spear down, extending it toward the prisoner treading in the water. The prisoner fanned off to the left and the guard took two steps to his right and leaned over again and extended the spear. The swimmer who was the black-haired woman's son hadn't made it very far, but we were still close enough to hear it all, the voices coming over the flat calm of the lake. The guard said to the prisoner, "Grab hold, I'll pull you up." The other guards had to laugh at that one. "Fuck you," the black-haired woman's son said, and in this case, I didn't mind the obscenity. You could hear in his voice that he knew he was going to die. You could hear the black-haired woman's voice in his voice, her maternity. The night before, the black-haired woman's son had looked down at the black-haired woman from his high prison tower and

DIVING INTO THE SUBMERGED
WITCH CEMETERY

—

Sometimes it's the sun up there, toothy, more consistent in its travel.

But usually it's the moon, rising bald and ladylike over the house-boat *Veronica*, just like it is now. Now we're anchored off an island the shape of a door-key about a mile South—or so the black-haired woman tells me—of the city of Port Sisterfield, the towers of the Penal Archipelago no longer visible in the distance.

By mothlight on the aft deck, the black-haired woman moves, small and fine, a pale black bird.

The boat sits still and light like a white plate on a black table.

—

The black-haired woman sallies back and forth, checking storage, opening traps. She glides like her feet are wheeled and seems to hand me a hand rake and a small spade. She points from beneath her hair, over the aft railing, at the black surface of the lake, the spot beneath which she believes to be the submerged witch cemetery.

"About there," she says, palming back her surf of hair, pink moths spilling out of it. The moths loop here and there around me, some of them dropping to my chest and torso to drink. I don't brush them away. I know my blood and the moths are part of it. "The sisters," the black-haired woman says, "if I remember right, straight down, about fifteen feet, not too lonely, all the way to the bottom. Use your headlamp," she says. "Keep your head up or the water will flood the helmet and then where will you be? You'll see the gravestones. Keep your eyes open," she says. She turns to look at me. "A bride should only close his eyes when he goes to sleep."

—

I know what a word like *bride* means. It means trust or something equally complicated, a map of skin. It means how the black-haired woman no longer thinks I will murder her, and therefore drinks benzene more than ever, smokes her living cigarettes, lets me find her passed out and unguarded in her fishing chair, passed out in the shower, lets me carry her, small and light, to her bed, whispering to me of an eventual murder that may or may not be mine. Maybe the word means vision, means the end of the masturbation booth. Maybe it means my murder is still a long way off. And would I want the murder now, I wonder, or later? Am I ready for the togetherness of it? Most probably with the knife or—as some stories of witches go—I will be eaten alive. Or both. But not tonight.

Tonight for the black-haired woman, and without a thought in my head, I will dive to the submerged witch cemetery. With a catfish spine for a pen, the black-haired woman draws symbols of protection, in the ink of freshwater squid, onto my back and my arms, what looks like a moon, what looks like a shell, what looks like the face of a person who has swallowed poison, and lastly, on my left palm, the head of a goat—I think the word is goat—its mouth open in song. Once again I wonder if there are really people in the world, or if it's just the black-haired woman and the boy she named as comrade. Where else might I have come from? Had the white-bearded gasman been real? And what about the black-haired woman's son, dead now? It worries me, too, that I'm also her child, that the story of my parents is just a story, that that's why I've been told the story, to make the life ahead viable, to keep me from running off and sentencing myself to the voluntary prisons. The human heart is much larger than the catfish heart. She steps back from me now to inspect the charms she's drawn. Then she steps forward again. With her fingertips she touches at the many raised moth bites on my torso, my chest. With the squid-ink quill and an empty look on her face she decides to connect the dots between the moth bites.

The constellation, when she completes it, is itself the shape of a star.

The very shape of it seems surprise her.

"Would you take a look at that," she says.

—

On the aft deck she shows me the diving helmet I'll wear down to the submerged witch cemetery, its brass fittings and exhaust pipes. I'm explained how the black panel on the topmost of the helmet traps the light of the sun for use. She points out the black snake of the tube running from the back of the helmet to the air pump, humped brass on the sistered decking. She sits on the cute-set deck chair, the air pump shiny at her feet, rehearses how she will work the air pump when I'm submerged, the long toes of her foot snugged around the handle of the lever, rocking the pump up and down.

"I promise to keep the air coming," she says, her black eyes sinking like tunnels into her head. This is a witch who has sometimes imagined my body sinking beneath the water, who looks at pornography of young men making love to purses and playing at being drowned. She snaps a match off the bottom of her foot and lights a crooked pink cigarette, gone wet-looking from the doings of the psychedelic insect life inside it. She shuts her eyes and her face drifts back, invisible, into her hair. She says, "The sisters are waiting. They don't mind waiting but they've waited long enough. Check around their torsos, under the armpits," she says, pointing out at the lake again, the spot beneath which the sisters had been buried, in their deaths before the flood or whenever, the flood before I was born. "Little pouches on lengths of twine or leather, little pouches on black bands," she says through pink smoke. "For the keeping of keepsakes," she says, "cats' teeth, knives without names, chicken grit, odd stones or the like, the lenses of the eyes of tiny fish, shiny breathing-bones, random jewelry, preserved moth bodies, finger and toenail charms, wee clay vials all full of what-have-you."

—

I step off the aft diving platform and drop into an automatic world, the mutter of moonlight through water and the underbelly of the houseboat *Veronica* looming above, a storm cloud. It's like the black-haired woman has said. By the bell of the diving helmet's light I can see the white silt of the lake bottom, down-slanting into the invisible cool of the lake, gravestones tilting here and there from the ridge like teeth come in badly, flashes of scale and fish belly at the far edge of the helmet light, even a great plated turtle easing off into the darkness. I imagine up to the aft deck of the houseboat *Veronica*. I picture the black-haired woman's foot working the hand pump in that silence, how she makes the air race toward me almost like from her body into mine, close enough, finding its way to my blood, to my fingertips and back. I feel like I'm a filter, a leaf soaking it in. In the diving helmet I carry the light of the single sun. I let myself drift to the nearest gravestone, hand rake in my hand, my shadow like a crab's.

—

I barely draw the rake across the first submerged grave before the long dead witch body, small and not even skeletal, pops from its resting place, its arms drifting forth to encircle my neck. It's like she's been waiting for me. The small face of this dead sister is wise and sleeping. Sometimes it's important to be afraid. The heartbreak-cut burial dress (no telling the color of the dress in that light, no one to say the color wasn't green) wavers flowerlike around the risen body. Lightly I hold the childlike form of the dead sister in my arms, so small. The diving helmet, heavy with the sun, presses us both to the silt. I've never had the chance to think while underwater. I don't have theories about life, as I've not been all that long in it, but I understand how, even if you're robbing it for a living witch, maybe it's not a good idea to rob the grave of a dead one. Therefore into the diving helmet I say a small prayer of due respect—"forgive me, but you are no longer alive"—and I lift the heartbreak-cut dress over the little witch's head.

—

Around the smallness of her torso I see it, through silt, a black band tight around the hips and a black cup, over where the belly button would be, like an eye patch for the belly button. I lift the cup of the eye patch from the witch's belly to check what might be beneath it. Not an extra eye alive and looking out at me—which I'd feared to see—nor even an emptiness, nor a little machine, nor is it now the lair of a sea creature and its eyes glowing out, nor is it love or war, Time or teeth neither, just a small pouch tucked for safekeeping in the minishaft of the belly button, held in place by the cup of the patch. I pull the pouch from the dead witch's belly button and I let go of the little body. It floats off into the darkness like a planet, feet over head, head over feet.

—

After a while of working underwater like this, my breathing fogs the glass of the helmet, revealing a secret message finger drawn by the black-haired woman, waiting there for my breath to have released it. The message says, simply, in the back-lean of her vibrating penmanship, "You are here." With these words between me and everything visible, I desecrate another sister grave, then another. The desecrations feel good, important, sanctioned by the black-haired woman. I feel large and unpunishable. Yet on the second and third unearthed sister bodies I find no other pouches, no other jewelry, no delicacies, no nothing, not even in the small pockets of the many small armpits. I desecrate a fourth grave, too, but there is not even a body inside it, just an empty dress. I breathe the air the black-haired woman pumps for me to breathe. I worry the witches I'm trying to rob have been robbed before. Happily I kick my way back to the surface when I feel the black-haired woman pull, three times, on the black air tube connecting me to the houseboat *Veronica*. I am here, but I am also there. And I am also, when you get down to it, the other way around.

WHITE HALF WORLD

—

On the stern deck now, where the moonlight is better, the black-haired woman kneels and looks at the little belly button pouch I've brought her, there in the palm of her hand.

"Could you read any of the gravestones?" she asks, not looking at me.

"No," I say. I stand next to her, dripping, breathing the new air. She pokes at the little belly button pouch with her forefinger. "She wore a kind of eyepatch over her belly button," I say.

"That's the old way," the black-haired woman says. In her palm the pouch looks like a black seedpod. I worry that my take is too small, but the black-haired woman seems pleased. "I really didn't expect you to find anything," she says.

—

She picks up the pouch between her two fingers and empties delicately its small contents onto the deck. There is a tiny clay vial, there is a small, barbed splinter of what looks like shiny black rock or metal, there is a tiny net of woven lake grass.

The black-haired woman picks up the small lake grass net and holds it between her fingertips. She looks through it, spreads it out. It isn't bigger than her eye. She sniffs at it.

"I don't know what that's supposed to be," she says.

—

Next she picks up the tiny clay vial. It fits small into the palm of her already small hand, a large bead. She holds her hand up to her face and looks closely at the vial. "It's still sealed," she says, her voice talking its harmony with itself. She smiles up at me young-like and with the tips of her fingertips she uncorks the minute vial. She sniffs at the tiny opening, at the cork. "I know what this is," she says. She stoppers the vial with her forefinger and upends it, on her fingertip now a little star-shine glisten. I lean down to better see.

"Open," she says, and I open my mouth. She hooks her fingertip along the inside of my lower lip. My mouth goes numb as a cave. Then my face. All I can feel are my teeth, strong like spikes I could bite through the boat with.

"Witch-spit," she says, looking again at the vial. "It came through centuries," she says, "just to wind up in your mouth."

—

"But this is the prize," she says. In her palm she holds the splinter of black rock, carved to a crescent-like arc, barbs on each end, like a piece of jewelry. The black-haired woman estimates this splinter as a tiny part of what had once been another planet. I sit down on the stern deck at her feet and wrap my arms around my knees to listen to what she has to say about outer space. The wind picks up and wheels the houseboat *Veronica* dizzily southward or northward. The boat pops at its anchor chain once, like a dog, before settling.

"A fragment of meteorite," the black-haired woman says. "With it," she says, closing her left eye in demonstration, "you were to pierce the eyeball, so that, once the eye heals, the subject can better see the invisible world. Demons and the like, or so it's said," she says.

"Or so it's said?" I say.

"Maybe demons," she says, shrugging. "Ghosts? I don't know. It's very old."

—

Later and destined I lie on my back, up on the balcony deck, looking for the moon that isn't there anymore. I hear the black-haired woman coming up the ladderway from the enclosed galley level. She steps over me and sits so that I can put my head in her lap.

"You lie there peacefully, almost like you're dead," she says upside down to me.

"Thank you," I say, her breath close, her face hanging over mine, constellations above.

"I find it very becoming," she says.

—

"What's your favorite color?" she asks.

"I don't know," I say. "I don't know all the colors."

"It's good to be patient," she says, "with bodies and colors and with other things." She holds my left eye open, touches her fingertip to the surface. My skull goes numb again from the witch-spit on her finger and she scoots back so she can hold my head still between her thighs. "I've never liked the word *eye*," she says. "Particularly when the word *eye* is written down, on a page, and I have to read it or am supposed to read it. I don't like how it feels when my eye passes over the word *eye*." I nod my head to say I know what she's talking about. She purses her mouth like she doesn't believe I know what she's talking about. "Right there above the iris of the left eye," she says, pointing to my eye as if I might not know where my eye is, showing me the black splinter, like a needle, between her thumb and forefinger. Now I begin to get the idea. "In an arc it goes in and over," she says, "just like a little black rainbow."

"Wait," I say.

"We can do this tomorrow if you want," she says.

"Tomorrow please," I say.

"Okay," she says.

Then she drives the splinter into my eye anyway.

Then the left half of the world goes white.

ONE MOON AND ONE SUN
AND ONE SKY

—

The night after the black-haired woman pierced my left eye with the ghost meteor, or maybe the night after that, I'm permitted to take a shower above decks, in the master bathroom, in the small coffin-sized shower. There I directed warm water over the hurt eye and lifted the serrated hunting knife from the shower shelf and tested its heft. I used a weird black soap. I dried myself off with a pink towel. I looked into the mirror over the sink, overall the eyes set too far apart in the head, just as the black-haired woman had described me a million times, but now with a black arc of meteor over the iris of the left eye. I couldn't say if there was anything going on behind those eyes. The more I looked the more I came to doubt it. I couldn't tell if the meteor in my eye held any magic, either, everything out of that eye just a little bit lighter, frosted in white. I felt new, changed, clean. I could hear the galley sounds of the black-haired woman cooking, drawers opening and closing. I could smell the catfish frying. I could hear the black-haired woman singing to herself and it made me feel like I'd been plugged in to something too powerful for my system, the dials and gizmos shaking loose from the chest. I was happy, in other words, that the boy who once looked like me was dead, that I was still innocent, or at least not at all jealous, yet, to be the unmurdered one.

—

On the galley table the black-haired woman set a pan of fried catfish and a plate of shining sliced tomatoes, purple in the meat. This
would be the first time I'd sit at table with the black-haired woman.
With her elbow she pushed a bowl of white sauce toward the middle of the table where we both could reach it better. She'd fried the
catfish lightly, still in their bones, doused them with lemon. The
meat was this clean and sugary mud and we ate very quietly, the
sound of insects ticking like small rain at the windows of the houseboat *Veronica*. It was dark out there, all the way out. You could feel
all that space rushing away from you like horses. Tendons popped
finely in the black-haired woman's jaw. I felt the boat was moving
again, though to where I never knew, humming along, the lights
of some sparse human shore off port. I chewed along in rhythm
with the black-haired woman. I watched her leave her fish bones
clean and stacked, like art, in a little pile at the edge of her plate. I
felt my heartbeat slow and I sank very quietly to a level of my brain
still being constructed. Beneath the table the black-haired woman
placed both of her bare feet on top of mine, as if to keep me there
if something unforeseen happened to gravity. She plucked a cherry
from the glass bowl of them and put it in her mouth and chewed.
She raised up and leaned her small body across the galley table. She
pinched my mouth open between her hands and spit the cherry pit
into my mouth.

A VISITOR II

—

That night with a cherry pit taking root in my stomach I slept alone and unmurdered in the small bed of the belly hold. I listened for sounds of the black-haired woman's footfall, hoping she might invite me to her bed, though also fearing it, what I might be asked to do and what would be done with me, if I would be found lovable, reusable, true. If it would be the end of this world or another. I had a cherry pit in my stomach and was becoming a world of my own. I also wanted to be a door that opened on something sunny and warm. But what would such a woman as the black-haired woman, a woman in such a boat, with knives in every room and every pocket, what would such a woman find desirable? Sun and warmth? I couldn't say for sure. So I looked up at the poster of the black-haired woman above the bed and I practiced how it might be when the black-haired woman came for me with her hands. I practiced my facial expressions. This was seduction in the age of one sun and one moon and one sky. I narrowed my eyes. I made my eyes wide. I made a face like I might be in the middle of having a pleasant dream and then I made a face like I was in the middle of being eaten alive.

—

Later toward dawn, with a soft-shell lake shrimp in my hand, I stood there, up in the galley, alone. Hungry I bit the head off the shrimp and listened to the high-pitched language of the bats, hunting the boat lights together in cheerful kill-teams. I could smell the body of the black-haired woman, asleep behind the door of her sleeping quarters. What I wanted to do was walk down the hall, kneel at the black-haired woman's door, and wait. But I just stood there, chewing. It would have been a nice quiet time to look back on my life, to think on what all had brought me to the black-haired woman, but I could remember nothing of my people or origins. My people were the black-haired woman, so much empty in me that there could be nothing to do but fill it.

—

The blue of the shrimp meat stained my fingertips.

I stood in the quiet of the galley and washed my hands at the sink.

I heard a little pop somewhere, below, and the lights went out, the galley going black.

—

In that dark I felt suddenly sick, like a bit of rotten ice broken off in my chest. A bolt of small silver lightning arced from my left eye, the meteor eye, shooting pretty sparks down into the sink and over my hands. I had the feeling that these sparks were my thoughts, leaking from the eye. I hadn't thought that sparks had weight but I could feel them hit my chest and hands, little shocks of pepper, outer space working through me. My knees buckled from the power of the eye and I turned around. And I turned around to see the white-bearded gasman crouching there, in the galley, where he was not supposed to be, dripping wet and still on the tile behind me, a twine-handled barbel-knife in his hand. How long had it been since he'd asked the black-haired woman for an hour with me? I'd forgotten all about him but he had not forgotten. He'd swum there from his gasboat to kill me or abduct me or both, to get more than an hour's say. I almost thought he was a piece of furniture come to life. The meteor in my eye covered him in a glowing silver light, pulsing as if he were a ghost.

The white-bearded gasman took a step closer. I pointed at him.

"You can't see me," he said.

"I can see you," I said.

"Lie to me again," he said, "and I'll turn your insides loose."

—

He stepped forward again so that our breaths touched each other and he tapped the point of the barbel-knife on the ledge of my belly button, letting it rest there. Gas and liquor came off him in waves.

"What's the story with your eye?" he asked.

I didn't answer.

"Which door is your pimp?" he asked.

"Who?" I said.

"Where does the sex witch sleep?" he asked. He tapped the tip of the knife back and forth to each interior side of my belly button.

"She doesn't sleep," I said.

He stood so close. His eyes were two different colors, but I can't remember which colors. This close they were beautiful eyes, really, above the false beard, buried treasure in the red-and-white ruin of his face.

"She sleeps," he said. "They all sleep," he said, like sleep was a failing in them, whoever they were, witches or black-haired women or both.

—

Maybe I felt immortal to hands other than the black-haired woman's hand. I wanted to tell the gasman, with my meteor eye, that he was dead. It was a little chill sweeping over my body, my nipples hardening to the warmth of the gasman's breath on my chest. And so it started. He pursed his lips like he would say to me a word that began with the letter B and I heard the black-haired woman crossing the galley on tiptoe, the little hoof taps as she sallied over the tile behind the white-bearded man. What came out of the white-bearded man's mouth was not a word that started with B but what first looked like a live thing, a shining beak rooting through the stained white of the false beard hair. I realized I was watching him die. He realized it too. In the embarrassment of his death the gasman passed his barbel-knife through the side-meat of my stomach, a second thought of pain for me, weightless and loose. The man spat his own blood into my face. Over his shoulder I could see the smallness of the black-haired woman, the bone handle of the knife in her hand, the babyfoot charm dangling and the tip of her knife appearing again from within the man's false beard, the elastic severed and the false beard slapping blooded onto the tile. The white-bearded man no longer had a white beard and he worked his mouth like a snake unhinging its jaw, the black-haired woman's knife gone home through the nape and throwing off the works in his throat. He dropped his own knife to the floor. I looked down and saw my blood on my belly and guessed I'd have dreams that night because of it, like the black-haired woman once said. Then the man wasn't there anymore but falling heavily over the snap of his own bones and I was looking into the face of the black-haired woman. She put her hand on my shoulder and brought her face close to me and stepped over the body she'd made. Silver sparks leapt from my meteor eye and the black-haired woman opened her mouth to catch them on her tongue.

"Your eye is so beautiful," she said.

—

We pulled the gasman's body from the galley, through the cockpit area and its photographs of young men making love to purses, then out onto the foredeck. She wanted whoever found the gasman's body to know she had caused the body, so she took off her heart-break-cut green dress and tied it to the dead man's foot. Everyone on the lake knew about her heartbreak-cut green dresses. Therefore the dress would mark the body with her authorship. It was important to put a body in the lake from time to time, she said. She stood nude as a stork on the deck and I tried not to look at her nakedness directly. She asked me to lift the dead man onto the railing, in a sitting position, his back to the lake. I perched him there, had to keep a hand on him to keep him from falling overboard. I've heard dead bodies spoken of as heavy, but I don't remember any heaviness, more I remember the slackness of the dead man's skin, almost mobile. The black-haired woman dressed an orange life preserver onto the dead man's body, so that he would float and be found dead even more easily. Then she chucked the head of a match along the underside of her foot and set the gasman on fire, his skin so fraught with gasoline that he went up with a whoosh that singed my eyebrows. I let go of him fast and he fell into the water, backwards, like falling from a window.

—

The black-haired woman sat perpendicular to me on a small green stool I hadn't seen on the foredeck before. Off starboard in the lake we could still see the gasman's burning body, floating off like a spirit lamp in the dark. The moon hung down low over the houseboat *Veronica* like it wanted to see what the black-haired woman might do next. I admit I was curious myself. She had a white rag on her knee and she didn't seem to feel sorry about anything. I wondered if she ever thought of the death of her son. I wondered if she thought of her own death, when that might be, if ever, if she was such a being as the white-bearded gasman, or instead some other being. It struck me that, before there might be a wedding, any wedding, it might be necessary for others to clear the world of their bodies, to make way, to let the earth lighten a little. I wondered if the gasman were part of some larger plan, or even the black-haired woman's son, or even the boy who once looked like me. The black-haired woman lifted the bottle of benzene and drank from it and didn't say anything about weddings or murders. Earlier she'd gone into her sleeping quarters and returned to the deck with the bottle and wearing a new heartbreak-cut green dress, her former dress now dangling from the ankle of the burning man's body, a treat for the fishes to look at. I'd thought I'd like seeing her without her clothes, but it only made me worry for her, in truth, her small allotment of skin, how it wasn't hiding anything it was built to hide, so I was glad of the new dress. Not that I didn't like the sight of her, for she was many-toothed and lightly boned and slim and powerful. It's just that she had seemed so vulnerable. She winked at me as if she knew my thoughts and she held up a needle in her hand and with one black eye shut she threaded it with a plucked strand of her black hair. The strand of her plucked hair looked the circumference of a noodle, seemed too big for the needle's eye.

With the excitement of the murder and the flaming burial at sea, at first the black-haired woman and I'd forgotten I'd been cut by the white-bearded man's barbel-knife. A lot of the blood on the deck of the houseboat *Veronica* was mine. The barbel-knife had parted the knot of my belly button, carrying right about an inch, little curds of fat and the revealing beach of muscle beneath. And now the black-haired woman explained how she would sew me shut, using her own hair as thread.

—

"If we're lucky he'll burn that way all night," she said of the gasman. We both looked out at the burning shape, disappearing in the dark distance. She held the bottle of benzene out to me and I took a drink. As always it tasted like something a volcano had waited a long time to say. Away from my wound she shooed the bloodthirsty moths of her hair, produced from the pocket of her heartbreak-cut green dress the roach end of one of her living pink cigarettes. The black-haired woman struck another match off the heel of her foot and she lit the cigarette and held it out to me.

"Just a little," she said, "or you'll be sick all night."

—

With the smoke of the bugs in my veins, I thought I felt my face get hot, but my face was miles away, up there where the moon was suddenly wearing it. I did feel a little sick, the twitch of bug tails in the narrow slot of the lungs, sick not in that exact specific dimension of space, maybe, but sick in another one. I mean to say I felt sick elsewhere. The black-haired woman raised and lowered the needle, the black thread of her hair running through me. The wound on my belly looked now like a small mouth half-closed, whispering out the side of its face. The black-haired woman had started the needle at the edge of the cut, worked her way back toward the belly button, tightening the thread of her hair until the edges of the wound touched again, drawing the needle up high above her head. I felt a little pain then, when she penetrated the cartilage, pain out to the fingers and toes, like a starfish. When I woke I woke to the black-haired woman holding open the lid of my meteor eye and looking down into it curiously.

"It's like you keep a little storm in there," she said.

DREAM AFTER SEEING BLOOD (THE GARDEN AT THE END OF THE WORLD)

—

Down another path and another I went in the dream, until I came upon a small garden, flowers and oblong moonlit vegetables, a black stream running through the garden, beside the stream a black bench, and on the black bench sat the black-haired woman.

"I thought you'd never find me," she said. She was her and she wasn't her. She wore a soft white dress, not green, not in the heartbreak but in the sundown cut, a white sundown-cut dress the black mass of her hair overpowered completely. I sat down beside her.

"Do you recognize this garden?" she asked.

"No," I said.

She looked around her, not quite with alarm.

"I don't think I recognize it either," she said.

—

She reached out, toward me, made her hand into a fist, used her fist to knock on my chest, like knocking on a door, and I looked down and saw that there was, just like that, a door there, leading to the heart, a door built into the chest, opening on the heart.

"That's new," I said, looking at the door to my chest. I was surprised the black-haired woman's dress was not green but white. I was surprised there was a door in my chest. I said to the black-haired woman, "Please don't open that door," but she was already opening the door.

—

"Shhh," she said, "or you'll frighten it." By "it" she meant my heart and she touched her fingertip to it. It was its own separate animal. I felt the roughness of the woman's finger on the heart wall, felt it also in the back of my throat, like her fingerprint had moved inside me.

—

"Wait a second," the black-haired woman said, "there's second door here."

I looked down.

And there was the second door, within, this one built in the wall of the heart itself, a door made of muscle, a little porthole, this one opening into the inner works of the heart. The black-haired woman opened this second door, as I understood she would, leaned and put her eye to the opening.

"So many rooms," she said, looking in, "servants, staircases, closets, chandeliers."

—

The black-haired woman stood from the black bench, let her white dress drop to the ground. When her white dress touched the ground, the black stream running through the garden turned white. Her face seemed worried, and she looked over her shoulder, as if afraid she was being watched. In this vision of her and maybe reality the head of her cock was heart shaped and she pushed in through the open door of the heart, which was my heart. She pushed inside and I saw the moon drop orange, like a hat, from the sky.

"Now I remember this garden," she said, her voice high above, though I could no longer listen. She said, "This is the garden in which you were born."

MARRIAGE IN THE TIME OF ONE MOON AND ONE SUN AND ONE SKY

—

I make this report because I know it's not everyone who understands what marriage is, or what happens before the marriage, during it, after, whether it is a state you enter or whether the state enters you, a state of being and having been in, or what a marriage opens up to you or what it shuts down, what is underneath it and above, or is it a corridor or a shaft, or let alone what could be inside it, what it's stuffed with, what fills it, if anything, and this is not even bringing into it the other person, to whom you are married, their interior, the matter of their filling. Or was it that you each filled the other? And was it something extra that you brought along? And about this other person: could you also say, then, that the other person, to whom you were married, was also married to you? Was it able to travel both ways? Could one say happily to the other: "You liked it." Or only did one person marry the other, like knocking that person out, stepping over them, then moving on to marry more? And which certain people were involved in this? Or even how many of them? All I knew was I had a feeling about the word *marriage*, a warm heat from the word alone, like holding your hand over a stove. And this much was clear, in my situation, at least: I knew the black-haired woman would decide, that I would be the one the word *marriage* flew toward, that I would fall, not off a cliff or over the side of a boat with my throat slit, or have a green dress tied to my ankle forever, but that's the kind of action I imagined, marriage: a falling, a happening, not necessarily a burial.

—

"I can tell you have questions about marriage," the black-haired woman said. We stood on the balcony deck in the moonlight. I knew I wasn't supposed to ask these questions about marriage, so I didn't. The moon was the one, the slightly-bigger-than-half one, the one that looked like someone took a bite out of a giant's left ear. The black-haired woman looked into my meteor eye. "You're going to make us very proud," she said.

—

"The pill is the best part of these weddings," the black-haired woman said.

I sat at the galley table, in the enclosed belowdecks, across from the black-haired woman, wondering how many brides she had had in her life, if any of them were still alive. For the wedding she wore black lipstick that made her lips seem sharper, her hands crossed at leisure behind her head, a puff of quiet black hair in each of her underarms, the citrus-and-licorice smell of her body. Sometimes witches murdered, sometimes they married. The black-haired woman leaned forward, and in the palm of her hand was a black, melted-looking pill, the magic she'd been talking about. I thought maybe she'd pulled the pill from her black hair, like a moth. It was more of a pellet than a pill. On the flat of her palm she showed it to me, closely. I reached out to take the pill between my fingertips. She closed her hand. I pulled my hand back. Then she opened her hand with the pill on the flat of it and held it closer to my face.

So I brought my head down to her hand, over the pill, like a horse.

"This is an excellent start," she said.

—

She caught my arm across the table and her hand was too strong and I sat back down. I hadn't meant to stand anyway. The pill made me able to see her face a little more clearly, which surprised me at first. There were indeed two eyes in her face, a single nose. The face was heart shaped, wide forehead, pinpoint chin. Those teeth. The triangle pink tongue behind the teeth. I decided she was beautiful. I decided this even though I wasn't positive what the word *beautiful* meant. The word seemed like a big world all on its own, a long stretch of territory.

—

"You'll want to lie down," she said. She'd say this to me many times in my life. By the time she finished saying it, this time, I was already in the act of laying down. I thought about her voice, hard and soft, the cool tile of the galley floor pressed against my cheek. She rolled me over onto my back.

"Now you'll have a vision," she said, "about the moment of your conception."

And I did. I had a vision of the moment of my conception, or what I thought was the moment of my conception. It was dark. I was a little thread of light in the belly of a mother, then the sudden molecules snooting around, snapping at me like a school of fish.

The black-haired woman stood over me, looked down. She seemed tall up there, dark clouds around her head.

"When your eyes close this time," she said, "you're going to disappear."

SOME MOTHERS

—

All that happened is I'd begun in the belly of an unknown mother. This was clear. And so had the body of that unknown mother (whose belly I'd ridden inside of) ridden within the belly of yet another mother, and that mother in the prior mother's belly, all the way back through time, birth in crypts, mothers burnt alive and bored to death, mothers putting their heads together and talking low so that no one else could hear. Did it matter which mother? There was nothing wrong with what the pill said of it. Maybe the fathers in the blood objected. I could feel their teeth rattling in my stomach. I'd seen the black-haired woman on the balcony deck of the houseboat *Veronica* without the excuse of her clothes. I was a single thing in a world of many dangerous things. And but now, in this place, whatever this place was, I was a boy who hadn't even been called a boy yet. It was a very young place. I wore pink shorts and the mothers came flying in through my mouth.

—

The milk of the first mother tasted like honey and dirt.

"Orphan Thing," the first mother said. She looked down at me, there in her lap, the play of the campfire on her face. The first mother looked, when I looked into her face, a lot like the black-haired woman, like her but younger. In the vision of the campfire, on dry land near caves and mouths of caves, the milk in my blood helped me feel the core of the earth, how it turned over twice in its sleep. I could sense what the low night clouds were thinking in their weird electric brains. They thought about how, between the earth and the sun, they were the only things alive. They didn't give a care about birds. They didn't think about the first mother. The first mother was young, younger than me even.

"Though I'm not the first mother exactly," the first mother said.

And so I thought it possible, with her reading my mind like that, that she might be Death. I looked up at her to check.

"I'm not Death, either," she said.

—

Sounds out there in the darkness, humans warring with monkeys in the trees. Everything was simple. There had even been a time in this place, I could feel, where nothing had died yet.

"Am I already married?" I asked the first mother.

"You're in the middle of it," she said.

—

"Things go so fast," the first mother said. "Soon enough," she said, "you have yourself a little grave. No one will hold your hand in it. The worms are your future relatives. The planet itself is a graveyard, basically. No one has been buried anywhere else."

"I never thought of it like that," I said.

"Every now and then you should do a little thinking," she said.

I tried to think up something I thought she might like to hear me say.

I said, "I sometimes get confused about who Death might be."

"So do I," said the first mother.

The moon moved quickly across the sky, more like a comet than the moon.

"Does the black-haired woman have a name?" I asked.

The first mother looked down, her black hair falling curtain-like.

"Who's this black-haired woman you keep talking about?" she said.

—

"I love what you've done with your eye," the first mother said. With her fingers she pried my left eye open. She leaned over and touched her tongue to its surface. What I felt was panic that I might be swallowed, eyes first, the long trip down the throat and the last thing I'd see. I sat up from her lap and faced her, my back to the campfire. She reached out and touched her finger to my belly button, stitched together by the hair of the black-haired woman. She said of the belly button, "This is where your mother was, but she isn't there anymore."

—

Sounds out there in the darkness, predators calling out to prey, then the prey calling out to me, like I might be able to do something about it.

I didn't know if I should say anything more to the first mother. The first mother didn't seem to know what to say either, but then she did say something. "Maybe I should call you *boy* now," she said, "before anyone else does."

"Yes," I said, "I think I'd like that."

CODICIL

—

I came out of it face up on the black-haired woman's huge white bed with a cherry pit under my tongue, the black-haired woman above me, silver fountain shooting up from my meteor eye, the sparks dropping down onto my nipples.

The huge white bed beneath me was beautiful like I imagined it would be, a cool stretch of meadow.

"You're like a bunch of fireworks," the black-haired woman said. She let the sparks of my eye fall into the palm of her hand. "Sorry if I woke you," she said.

"It's okay," I said. "I'm very glad to see you."

—

She sat back from me on her knees. She pulled her hair up out of her face with both hands and she made her hair into the shape of a rocket, a boat, an elephant. She fanned at her neck with her hand and looked over at her shadow on the wall.

"How does it feel to be the bride?" she asked.

"It feels like I'm in an ancient story," I said.

"You're not half wrong," she said.

"Is this the first time?" I asked.

"I'm losing count," she said.

—

I reached up and put my hands on her shoulders, cupped the thin tower of her neck. On the wall to my left I could see the small shadow of the black-haired woman's body moving above the large shadow of my own.

"You spoke in your sleep," she said.

"What did I say?"

"It wasn't words really," she said. "But it wasn't music either."

—

I slipped off, saw the first mother again in a brief flash, from a distance, her poking at her campfire idly with a crooked stick, then I returned to the black-haired woman, as she was in the Now, her face in my face, her eyes wide open as she moved against me. This close she was smaller of body than ever. She looked at me like I was something spilled from a net at her feet. She locked one hand around my throat so she could better concentrate on her leverage. I looked down at the shot of pink glitter on my stomach and I knew it was time to invent the word *love*.

HONEYMOON IN BLACK

—

Then came long days without (yet) murder, fruitfulness and disease without worry, pink glitter chevrons on my cheekbones, the affection of three-and-twenty brides bound and hung upside down from a bar in my heart, knees and long days of catfish slime and trout oil, waking up confused in the pitched terrarium of her black hair, hearing her talk in her sleep to whichever ghosts the black-haired woman might talk to, waking to find strands of her hair wrapped as ribbon around my genitals, pulling her hair from my mouth and from my eyelashes and from my food, laying quietly while she removed the stitches from my belly button with her teeth, drunk afternoons in swim fins along the deepest edge of the Great Trout Weedbed, diving down the green and purple stalks of that underforest with a fillet knife in hand for the tender white berries that grew on the flower buds five feet down, careful eye for the freshwater shark, the black-haired woman diving in the nude, the two of us breathless on the deck of the houseboat *Veronica* as if we'd met in a different world, too many worlds in general, benzene in my heart like opening a large box to find a smaller box inside it, kneeling bedside in that warm feeling during rainstorm while the black-haired woman figured the slant of my throat, told me of the way the world would end (without animal or plant on it, apparently, and human flesh on it only: cannibalism, hand-holding,

fear of robots coming to fuck us, fear of robots without condoms),
lock and key until I thought my head would open like a music box,
days lying in bed with the black-haired woman while she showed
me photos of her favorite pornographies, "That one," she would say
of the purse in the photo, "the one with the puppet-skin trim," or
she would say, her fine finger hovering over a photo of a young man
on his knees before a great green purse large enough to contain a
forest, "That one, the one with the secret compartment inside the
secret compartment," the black-haired woman feeding me sticky
black pills so she could be alone with my body without me in it, me
somewhat jealous of that body alone with the black-haired woman, wondering what she said to that body, if she said love talk to
it, if she told it where the moon was and what the moon looked
like, days worried about how much taller I was than her, always
a surprise to see the hulk of my own body's shadow next to the
witched-down slimness of hers, so narrow at the waist the shadow blurred out at her middle, days wondering what season it was
and if Winter would ever come or was Winter always a myth, days
of wondering how many days there would be, days with my head
wrapped in the black-haired woman's sheets while she attacked the
body without the head, the shape of her breath in my ear saying
"terraform" and "stubble," my meteor eye firing sparks to the ceiling,
fried fish and dried fish and smoked shrimp in the galley, days in
receipt (unbeknownst to me) of the black-haired woman's allotted
venereal disease, for this was her wedding gift, there's something
to be said for venereal disease, finally the body under attack from
within after having lived lonely and golden for too long (more on
venereal disease later), for now just meeting the need of the circuit,
again and again, on my knees now on the balcony deck with her
pink moths fluttering about me, on my knees in the black dirt of
the tomato garden, on my knees in the shower looking into the

keyhole of her belly button, looking between my legs upside down and under the balcony railing to see the tendons in her feet straining, taut and fine like the cords of a toy piano, her body so small she stood on boat cushions to be tall enough, great days wherein I felt myself the buffer between the black-haired woman and the invisible world she searched through for evidence, picnic of braised lake snails and unknown wine on a raft floating just off the beach of Governor's Island (for the black-haired woman would not set foot on land, not even to picnic), me on my back in the raft and the meteor eye going off in both our faces like a misfire and her hair scorched and smoking, pink and glitter and the lemon and the knife, the hardness of her long toes puncturing the raft, looking up at the sun past the triangle of the black-haired woman's face, wondering what kind of mother I would be if the black-haired woman ever made me into a mother, not too clear on boy biology or anyone's biology, the feeling, anyway, that her children were loose in me already.

THE LIVING DOTS

—

Though in some ways her children were loose in me already.

She said: "There are many venereal woes sovereign to Crescent Lake." She stood from her cute-set deck chair and stepped toward me, balcony deck, my hands at my sides so that she could describe me, the sun rising slowly but continuously, as if by pulley. Southlike on the lake I could see a white shrimp trawler motoring in the general direction of the houseboat *Veronica*, its nets tucked up high like wings, its nose bent to one side. The black-haired woman looked out at the trawler then lowered her head of hair and touched her finger to a small white dot there on my inner thigh, high up. These dots were new since the honeymoon. She pointed out another dot, up toward the belly button, near the still-reddish punctuation of the gasman's scar. She pointed out another dot right above my cock, this dot angry with a couple of (what looked like) black feelers poking through the skin. She ran the rough of her fingertip back and forth across the feelers. I drew back, little slivers in the nerve, a wriggle in the back of my actual throat.

"First there's the Bloodbath," she said, listing off venereal woes. She said, like she was talking to someone other than me, "Obviously he doesn't want the Bloodbath. And then there are the Shudders, which are very cold and lonely. Then there is the Sweet-Grass Tickle, which is a rash and a bad dream. Then there's the one they call the Visions, which is an infection of the aura and of the genitals. There are many others, the names of which I have forgotten. But the venereal woe I've given you," she said, touching her finger to her tongue, rubbing her own actual witch-spit onto the feelered red dot, "is the Living Dots. The Living Dots aren't so bad except for how they are alive. Most everyone around here has had the Living Dots. The bumps go from white to red, then your teeth loosen, and then, eventually, the bugs come crawling out on their own, though what we're going to try to do here," she said, smiling up at me, "is see if we can get them to come out a little faster. And if we can get them to come out a little faster," she said, "then we will smoke them in a nice pink cigarette."

—

Face up on the balcony deck, feeling the living things inside me, I heard the whinny of the approaching shrimp trawler's engines. The trawler blew its horn to hail us and the black-haired woman waved at the trawler absently. She knelt beside me, holding a lit match to a length of carbonated black wax. I thought how, since the black honeymoon, she'd come to look younger, thinner, even more narrow. Her black hair kept the sun from my body and in that shadow made by her hair she showed me the tiny round scars between her legs, so that I could see how the Living Dots weren't so bad, particularly when managed, when farmed. She blew out the match and stamped the hot butt of the wax onto the dot up near my belly button. The wax felt nice, soothing, but the bug in there didn't like it, rolled over inside me, sharpening its beak.

"You're like a world and a world has animals," she said.

"I can feel it moving inside me," I said.

"It doesn't want to die," she said. "It wants to see the sun."

"I think it's coming out."

"Yes," she said, "I can see its little eyes."

—

One after the other she tricked the bugs out of me and placed them wriggling in my belly button for safekeeping. Each pulled insect left behind an angry crater in my skin and the black-haired woman licked her finger and touched her finger to each crater, soothing it with her spit. When she kissed me it was like this too, with her spit, my lips and face going numb. The bugs skritched and wriggled in the cup of my belly button and the shrimp trawler circled us, getting a live sighting of the black-haired woman, famous to this lake.

The black-haired woman made a face at the trawler, a hand-gesture. "For such a vision as this must be," she said, "I ought to charge them money."

—

From her hair she produced a pack of pink rolling papers and tore one in half to make a smaller cigarette. I had only brought forth a small harvest of insects. One by one she pinched the insects from the cup of my belly button and spilled them onto the paper and twisted the paper at both ends. The little bugs that had been inside me wriggled now in the pink rolling paper. She popped a match off her heel and drug from the cigarette and she held the smoke in. Her teeth moved in unison in her mouth and her head lolled a little.

"It's best like this," she said, "fresh from the body."

—

Then followed love-act on the balcony deck with the bugs gone up in smoke, my internal organs pressed too close together and black wax flaking off me like scabs. Beneath the black-haired woman I felt how it might feel to be in outer space, trying to work back through the atmosphere and home, that or I was the atmosphere.

"I chased the animals from you," the black-haired woman said, my head crooking up underneath the tomato plants of the balcony garden, the sun coming through them green while the bent-nosed shrimp trawler circled us. The black-haired woman had many fans on Crescent Lake, apparently many fans on this shrimp trawler, whose captain kept his boat in a tight spiral around the houseboat *Veronica*, so that his crewmembers might see for themselves what they had so long heard rumors about, which was the fashion of the black-haired woman's lovemaking. Through the patchwork of the tomato leaves I could read the trawler's name as it passed on its loop, the *Harm and Foam*. The black-haired woman spoke to me, down through the leaves, her head of black hair like a buffalo, her talk about how I couldn't hold a baby for her, but how biology shouldn't make anyone cry about it, talking how the men on the trawler boat were jealous of me, that and other things she said— about my chest, about my flexibility—things that made me feel sweet, eventual, and real. The men on the deck of the trawler *Harm and Foam* cried out to us, over the waves. They put their eyes on me like hands. They cheered for the black-haired woman, to see the strength of what she did, though I could feel in their voices their envy. They would not mind switching places with me, maybe like you, yourself, dear reader, or like anyone would, wearing the pink shorts, becoming a farm, *love* a word you use carefully so as not to be made dead, riding on a boat in tune with stars. In tribute and over the railing of the *Harm and Foam* the trawlermen tossed the little bodies of turquoise shrimp onto the balcony deck of the houseboat *Veronica*. They rained down shrimp and weedflower and small coins. I looked up at the underside of the tomato leaves, the jungle of the garden, and there I also saw, for the first time, little green worms beneath the leaves, an infestation glowing green and red, eating at the tomato fruit, their unknown diligence. What with the black honeymoon I had not kept up the care of the garden and now there were worms in it. These worms were everywhere. I reached up to pluck one from its leaf, but before I could, it dropped from its weight and fell on my chest.

"Not yet," the black-haired woman said. She punched the flat of her palm on my chest, crushing the worm, smearing it across my skin.

A FEW NOTES ON THE CARRYING
OF WITCHES

—

Sometimes a witch might be thinking she's going have a bad night. She'll walk off in her heartbreak-cut green dress and she probably won't say "I love you." She will be thinking of the lifetime of murder she's had commit in order to stay a witch, to stay alive. She will wonder how to put the bugs in you and then to smoke them. She will wonder if she can still murder with any kind of tenderness after all this time. And instead she will ask you from the corner of one black eye, over her shoulder as she leaves the room, "Are you still vibrating?" And then she will leave you in the belly hold to think about what's expected of you.

—

Sometimes a witch drinks too much and smokes the living cigarettes all afternoon, particularly when the witch in question trusts you not to murder her. In some ways she's been looking a long time for a person like you. It's hard in this world for a human to find another human they can trust and say a simple truth in front of, let alone a witch. Witches have a harder time of it.

—

Sometimes when a witch is drunk she'll say, "Your sheep are your voice." She will ask, "Why do you expect magic from me?" She will send you to the belly hold to think about what good might ever come of you.

—

When a witch passes out, loses her own consciousness, you feel it in your heart, a little tickle in one of the four spoken-of chambers, where her spells have roosted. You can feel it in your joints, a slight ache in your hips. You get up from your bed in the belly hold and scratch the bumps between your legs and then you search the boat longingly for your witch.

—

If your witch is found passed out on the bed in her sleeping quarters, then you've found your witch where she's supposed to be. You should kiss her forehead and leave her to herself. But if she is not found where she's supposed to be, then you must find her elsewhere and return her to the spot where she's supposed to be, which is her bed.

—

If not found on her bed, then, she will be found on the balcony deck, beneath the umbrellaed table, curled up with a knife in her hand, the babyfoot charm in her mouth as pacifier. She will be found on the floor of the coffin-sized shower with the shower mat pulled over her for blanket. She will be found slumped over in the captain's cockpit, her forehead pressed to the console, for she is the captain but she is also a witch. She will sometimes write a note for you, in her levitating hand, pin it to her chest for you to discover when you discover her. The note will say, "If found, please return to bed," or "Murder is not a failure of the imagination." And you will roll this note into a little ball and swallow it. You will lift the body carefully and you will not be surprised by how light the body is.

SOME IDEAS ABOUT WHO VERONICA MIGHT HAVE BEEN, PLUS A SECOND ESCAPED PRISONER, PLUS MEMORIES OF OCCASIONS WHEN THE BLACK-HAIRED WOMAN HAS ENTERTAINED LOVERS ON THE HOUSEBOAT *VERONICA*, PLUS A SMALL CAPTURE OF TOADS

—

"I don't know who Veronica is, or was."

She sat, lightly hungover, folding in on herself beneath a black parasol, the black greasepaint under her eyes making her look even more singled out by the universe, high on the conical cigarette that burned forgotten between her knuckles, the conical cigarette which now included bugs born out of my body.

This was deep into Summer 2, maybe the beginning of Summer 3.

I watched her smoke the living cigarette and twirl the parasol and I thought of the slenderness of her lungs. There weren't calendars around, except the Living Dots themselves, the psychedelic bugs that come on like a calendar inside me. I got so I could taste their arrival in a kind of bitterness on the flat of my tongue. I walked the boat with my hair tender, my teeth loosening in the gums, until my breath (back and forth) made the teeth in my mouth sway like reeds. I'd had a series of dreams where my teeth fell out of my mouth like spent cartridges, black feathers rising from the sockets in place of teeth, and I worried that these dreams meant change. I didn't want to change. I didn't tell the black-haired woman about these dreams. I'd hoped to achieve a kind of permanence, in front of her, either living or dead.

—

The sun rose huge above us, an emergency the sky was throwing. In the cool shade of her black eyes I knelt half leaning over and into the tomato garden, hunting with my hands for the hooked red-and-green worms I'd seen in there when the trawler *Harm and Foam* had been circling us, worms eating their code into the silver-haired tomato leaves. The garden was my responsibility, and the advent of the worms struck me as a failure. They hung from the under leaves like little parcels. They'd grown so fat they made the leaves droop with their weight.

"There are too many of them," I said.

I unhooked one, dropped it on the deck. The black-haired woman ended it with her heel.

"There was a man," she said, flicking the guts off the bottom of her foot, "who owned the boat before I owned it. I suppose Veronica was someone important to this man. A mother of his, a lover or a daughter, or whatever else a person named Veronica could've been."

—

"Sometimes I even forget," she said, "what your name is."

She looked me in the face, as if she'd catch me in a lie.

"You named me," I said.

"So you keep saying," she said.

"Orphan Thing," I said.

She nodded. She looked off into the distance. "Orphan Thing," she said.

—

Then there was the day of the second escaped prisoner.

On that day we'd motored from the bay of Port Sisterfield toward the islands of the Knee Keys. She stopped the boat in a clear bay whose bottom lay dotted with what looked like little meteors. The black-haired woman threw her cast net for the forobosco that swam there in roiling silver hives, her body sharp under the heartbreak-cut dress, her bunched net sailing high, blooming into a circle. I liked to watch her engaged in a job of work, her muscles, her angles. She filled the live wells with these fish (whose raw flesh went so well, she said, with a sip of benzene) and then she motored the *Veronica* on down the lake, and that evening, beneath a sun falling apart in fruity chunks, we saw a man sitting on a rock island, shading his eyes and looking at us. This man wore the orange jumpsuit of the voluntary prisons, but unzipped to his belly button, his broad shoulders pink with sun.

—

After the man swum from the rock island to the *Veronica*, he sat cross-legged on the foredeck, dripping and male, and shared the black-haired woman's benzene.

He was a smaller person than me in height, yet wide and packed with muscle.

He turned down the sliced tomatoes I brought out to him on a little plate.

He wore a false black beard for the masculinity of it.

"Do you think we'll have ourselves a Winter this year?" the man asked.

The black-haired woman ignored his small talk and went straight to the point.

"Maybe you mean to murder me," she said.

"No," he said.

She knelt for a closer look at his face and she took the bottle from him.

"You stink," she said.

"I've been in prison for a while."

"Take that moronic beard off," she said.

He unstrung the beard, placed it carefully next to him, like it was a pet he worried for. His bare face looked odd, caught doing something it shouldn't. He looked over at me and nodded. The black-haired woman watched his eyes. "That's Orphan Thing," she said.

"We heard rumors about a marriage," the man said.

"I guess they know who I am in that prison," she said.

"Yes they do," he said. "You have a lot of fans there."

"What do they call me?" she asked.

"They call you the black-haired woman," he said. He turned his face away. "Maybe some other things, but I won't repeat them."

"Uh-huh," she said. She said, "And what do *you* call me?"

"I don't believe I ever called you anything," he said. "I've just thought a lot about you, at night very often, but also other times."

She sat origami-like on the foredecking in front of the new man who was our guest. She pointed her toes and she showed him the sickle-bladed suit knife with the babyfoot charm.

"Ever seen one?" she asked.

"I've seen ones like it," he said.

"It's," she said, "a knife."

"I don't doubt it," he said.

They sat there, looking at each other, at the knife in her hand. I got the feeling I should probably stand up and make myself scarce. In a little she hid the knife in her heartbreak-cut green dress and leaned back, putting her feet in the man's lap. The man looked down at her feet. The black-haired woman didn't say anything.

"For the record, I'm not looking to die, or at least it's not at the top of my list," the man said. He almost touched her feet with his hands but then he didn't know if he should. He said, "I'm not looking to die but I'll risk it. I hoped it would be you who found me. I know the *Veronica*, the black-haired woman, the green dress. I've watched you from the prison towers, and I've sung to you at night with the rest of them. I hoped it would be you who found me, not one of the incest boats you see around here, nor the guard boats, of course, nor some deckful of dirty trawlermen."

"I know a lot of dirty trawlermen," she said.

"I don't mean any offense," he said. "I just mean I know this boat. I'm glad I'm here and not all the other places I could've wound up."

—

"Why did you sentence yourself to prison?" the black-haired woman asked.

The escaped prisoner smiled a soft smile that showed us how his two front teeth had been attempting, over time, to switch places. They formed a lazy X, the right crossed over the left. He said, "I had a small daughter and a slightly larger son. But I wasn't very good at it. My wife didn't have to tell me about it. I knew I wasn't a father. I just didn't worry about them at all, or have dreams in which I imagined myself having to save them from this peril or that. I didn't feel protective in the least. They hardly seemed made out of my own skin. The boy would play with matches and guns and I'd just laugh. The girl would go off with disreputable characters and I'd tell her to have a good time. I couldn't bring myself to have concern. There was something like a failure in me."

The black-haired woman nodded. "Children can be strange," she said.

He looked at me. He looked at her. He said, "I knew your son, by the way."

—

"That was too bad when he died," she said. She drank from the benzene and belched faintly.

"I spoke to him before," the man said. "The night before he swam. He sure was sorry that he left you back when he did. But at the same time," the man said, "I don't think he knew what else to do about it."

"That sounds like him," she said.

"Anyway," he said.

—

"Do you have a name?" she asked.

He waved his hands. "No," he said.

"Names aren't as important as they used to be," she said.

—

"Did you ever have the Living Dots?" she asked.

"Of course," he said. "Everyone gets the Dots. I've been alive all this time, haven't I?"

"You tell me," she said.

The man didn't know what to say to that so the black-haired woman carried on.

"Anything else you'd like to claim?"

"I had the Visions once, but a witch in Torsion Cove cured me of it."

"I wasn't aware of a cure."

"You know how cures are," he said. "Some people remember a cure, some people don't. It's hard to keep a common history of such things."

The black-haired woman liked this answer. She leaned back, holding herself lightly up with her palms against the foredeck.

"And so you've brought yourself here," she said, "to let me decide what's to become of you."

"I guess that's right," the man said.

The black-haired woman crossed her feet and tapped her big toes together.

"Take off the jumpsuit," she said to him, "and let me describe you."

—

Because she wanted to be alone when she showed the second escaped prisoner the fashion of her lovemaking (and also possibly when she murdered him), and because she worried (like I did) about the translucent red-and-green worms infesting our tomatoes in the garden on the balcony deck, that evening the black-haired woman sent me out on the raft with a spirit lamp and a burlap sack (for the keeping of any toads I might catch to put in the tomato garden) and I paddled toward the nearest of the Knee Keys, feeling very strange to be suddenly alone, feeling strange to see the houseboat *Veronica* behind me, behind me and without me on it, big hook of wood on the water. From the point of view of the raft, the houseboat *Veronica* looked large and white, weather-beaten, whereas if anyone had asked me, I probably would have described the *Veronica* as a pink boat, glitter in the paint. I hadn't very often seen the houseboat *Veronica* from anywhere but *on* the houseboat *Veronica*. But there it was, a fact, the boat not pink but a certain battered white after all, the raft I paddled from it leaking slowly from the hole the black-haired woman's feet had punched in it during the floating picnic of the black honeymoon, which already seemed like years ago. As I paddled the raft, it became necessary to pause every so often and lower my head to the raft's air valve and blow so that the raft wouldn't sink beneath me. I paddled and blew, paddled and blew. It was the first time, that I could recall, that I'd ever been alone, or at least without the black-haired woman somewhere nearby. The island I paddled toward was a small island, but to me it seemed the world, huge and busy, waiting for me patiently.

—

I could've named the island upon which I spent that night with my spirit lamp while the black-haired woman and the escaped prisoner lay together alone on the houseboat *Veronica*. I could have named it, but I didn't, fearing that whatever name I came up with might be too troubling to recall in the future. I wasn't always sure what tone my memories would be cast in. Names didn't matter all that much those days, anyway. On shore, in view of the houseboat *Veronica*, I set the spirit lamp alight in a clearing among pine trees. I sat leaning with my bare back against a tree, fighting the mosquitoes that were worse than bloodmoths, the burlap sack ready in my lap. I tried not to listen to the sex act on board the houseboat *Veronica*, but it was a calm night, the harmony of the black-haired woman's voice saying small things over the flat of the water, the sounds of the escaped prisoner as the black-haired woman decided what would become of him, so close it was like she was whispering in my ear and not his, and how at one point he sounded like he had been levitated, how at one point he sounded like the black-haired woman had cut his voice into different little voices so that all of them spilled from him at once in little wriggles, how he hollered at one point "Your hair is bigger than me," and things like "I see the fossil of a star," or "I finally know how I've been alive all this time." Things like things you might say, lucky, with a witch in your face. I sat with my back against the pine and watched the halo-cast of the spirit lamp for approaching toads that might have interest in the winged insects attracted to its glow. I worried about larger animals, too, like the wolf or the lion, afoot on the island. This was not the first time, I didn't think, that the black-haired woman had entertained others on the houseboat *Veronica*. I'd had my suspicions for a while. Let me speak about these suspicions. On those nights when I woke with the black-haired woman speaking odd words to my body and making guttural shapes with her hands, sometimes I'd fallen into the deep sleep her words and gestures designed for me, but other times I lay awake in half of a stupor, only partly full of the charm, listening to the phantom shape of what went on above decks. Maybe a handful of times, with the houseboat *Veronica* anchored off the bay of Port Sisterfield, or in the narrows leading to the whorehouses of Torsion Cove, I believed I'd heard important noises. The sound of oarlocks squeaking on the flat of the water, new footsteps on the foredecking, the thump of one boat together with the hull of the *Veronica*, a rendezvous, whispers of congratulations from the black-haired woman, different voices answering her back, laughing with doom and warmth. Yes, I think she met with lovers, who swam to her or came to her in small boats from the mainland, sun ones and moon ones, male ones and even otherwise, all above me on these bridal nights, the sound of the black-haired woman's enjoyment of these invisible bodies, the hoof-tap of her toes on the deck and parts being used for what parts might be used for. It wasn't something that I minded, I don't think, not the act itself, not the others as others. I only worried over my place in such things, worried that I might not be her bride for very long. Worried that she might murder me and move on, even though, to some extent, her murdering of me (I had to admit this to myself, finally) was what I wanted, love and murder circling each other, the togetherness of that act, not necessarily to die but to be killed in mid-flirtation. I don't know how many brides she'd taken in her life, nor how many might be left alive. And now, across the water as I listened, I heard the escaped prisoner say something like "I still don't know which side is the starboard side," and you could hear the black-haired woman laugh at that. She didn't laugh a whole lot in her life. I admit the sound of it, now, alone on the island, affected me, her hard laugh underneath her soft, the freedom in her voice, the delighted sound she made toward the end of her pleasure in him, like falling down a ladder, but happily, a noise she'd made sometimes with me, her face in my face, and then everything going quiet for a while across the lake, which is when I saw the little eyes of the toads twinkling at the edge of the circle of the spirit lamp's light, two pair, three pair, coming for the flutter of insects that were their joy. I leaned forward with the burlap sack at the ready, crawling. I whispered into the short handsome face of each toad how it wasn't an abduction. I would be doing them a favor. There was a fine tomato garden on the houseboat Veronica, full of red-and-green worms, fat and wracked with the heat of Summer 3. I crept forward on my hands and knees. "You don't know it yet," I whispered, "but it's going to be a paradise."

LIKE GHOSTS WITH A LITTLE PINK LEFT IN THEM

—

Said the black-haired woman: "Don't step on my shadow."

I moved my foot.

"Apologies," I said.

—

She touched with her fingertip each of the teeth in my mouth, assaying.

"They're tightening up," she said of the teeth. "I don't really think you'll lose any."

"Did you murder the escaped prisoner?" I asked.

"I can't remember," she said.

"How many murders have there been?"

"In the world," she said, "or belonging to me?"

"To you."

She knelt down. "Move your body only very little," she said.

"Like this?" I asked.

"That's good," she said. "Look at me," she said.

"Where's your face?" I asked.

"Adjacent," she said.

"What do you look like?" I asked.

"None of your business," she said. She said, "Here, I want to show you something."

"What is it?"

"What will you think?"

"It doesn't look familiar," I said.

"S'okay what it looks like."

"Am I supposed to feel dizzy?"

"If you feel dizzy."

"It feels like swimming," I said.

"It feels like falling through a bridge."

—

"How many murders belong to you?"

"I don't remember them that way," she said. "Most of them I forget because they were not that important. Some of them I remember because they were full of a certain tenderness." She poked my ribs with her toes. "Mainly," she said, "I remember if it was day or night. And I remember the weather. Most often it was during the night," she said, "but about a dozen happened during the day. About six happened with no clouds in the sky. (Open your mouth.) But most times with clouds. Then one time on an island beneath big white clouds that looked like cathedrals and one time with clouds that looked like big white underclothes. Fourteen times during rainstorms. (Touch your tongue to the roof of your mouth.) Then one time I looked up and saw a double rainbow. Once during a solar eclipse and twice during a lunar eclipse and fifteen times when the moon was full. (Make a noise you've never made before.) Then once during a typhoon, though that was a double murder. (Point your toes like in dancing.) It hasn't snowed around here in some time, but three times when there was snow on the ground. (Say a little prayer to yourself. Don't let me hear it.) Then once when a meteor crushed the governor's house on Governor's Island. Twice during tornadoes and once during an inverted tornado and once during a sandstorm that came from the other side of the world— (you can close your mouth now)— to see me with a knife in my hand."

—

Though I lived already as a bride there were some ways I was a virgin still, as I have said one thousand times, as I will go on to say. Later that night, with the moon far like a button, the black-haired woman explained it all in more detail, part biology, part magic, part alarm, part invasion. In Torsion Cove, where she would send me, I could be used by others, others in the way that she used me, but I couldn't use anyone myself, same way it was between me and the black-haired woman herself, one person doing the flying, the other person still, like a tree. On a piece of scrap paper she drew a little diagram for me, showing me what *use* meant. She double wrapped one of her hair ties around my genitals, cordoning them off, further sending the message. I was a hairless gift from the mostly understood universe, and so forth. I'd enter only water and buildings. I was a staging area but I couldn't stage anything.

"Do you know what I mean?" she said.

—

One evening we stood on the foredeck, now anchored in deep water off the narrows leading to Torsion Cove. The black-haired woman didn't set foot on land, so I would set foot on land for her. Land was where the money was. With the dark trees looming up over it, the cove looked more like the mouth of a cave. Spirit-lights hatched along the shores of the narrows and the docks, the less-steady signal of campfires up in the hills behind the homemade profile of the settlement, the burly sound of voices, a tangle of musical instruments, the reedy cry of bobcats mating in the bush. You could make out a couple of buildings from our vantage on the decks of the houseboat *Veronica*. The black-haired woman pointed them out to me. Here the mayor's house central with its peaked roof, there a couple of shacky structures that may have been eating or sleeping establishments—it had been a long time since the black-haired woman had walked through Torsion Cove—and then of course the loose-limbed shadow that was the famous building called the Oligarchy, dominant with its two corrugated stories and a wraparound porch, the goal of lonely trawlermen.

—

Around nightfall—I was up on the balcony deck, practicing with the bang-knives, feeling the tiny explosions in my hand, firing the blade into a couple of rotten tomatoes I placed on the balcony table—an air horn sounded from the settlement of Torsion Cove, followed by a brief crinkle of applause. From the *Veronica* you could see people moving in profile on the docks, stopping, turning landward to look at something. The black-haired woman stood below me on the foredeck, eating from a plate of sliced tomatoes.

She had her hair wrapped up in a white towel and her face was terse and quiet. The air horn sounded again and she turned and looked up at me.

"Watch the hills," she said.

—

The prostitutes of Torsion Cove: now one by one they came flying. The black-haired woman pointed up into the hills at the flickering of the campfires distant there. She explained what was happening and the explanation failed to drain the happening of its mystery. Up in the hills, from the scattered campfires down to the roof of the Oligarchy, ran a series of light zip lines, or so the black-haired woman described. I could neither see the lines nor the platforms from that distance. I trusted how the black-haired woman spoke of it. Each night when the air horns blew, the sun ones and moon ones would strap themselves onto the zip lines and push off, their pink shorts and pink dresses cutting through the air, as they were doing now. I watched it happen, pink comets streaking down from the hills from seemingly nowhere, the hills giving up their optimism to the town. People in the settlement below and along the docks all cheered. I looked at my pink shorts. I looked back at the hills, pink-clad bodies coming down the lines, one after the other, as many as the petals of a flower. They looked like pretty birds swooping over the dark-green canopy, small but getting larger and larger as they sailed over the rooftop of the Oligarchy, dropping to the roof to do their job of work for the evening, not flowers or birds or ghosts, but human. They fluttered down from their many points of origin, but all landed in the same place. They stood together along the edge of the roof, arms around each other, greeting each other as each new friend landed. You could see how they enjoyed seeing each other. You could see how they bowed and curtseyed to the small crowd of patrons forming a line below.

THE OLIGARCHY, THE WOMAN ANNE SEXTON 3, A STUDY OF FACIAL HAIR, A GIRL NAMED COZILLA

—

From the low ceiling of the Oligarchy, on varying lengths of monofilament, hung small taxidermied birds of different colors, frozen in attitudes of flight. Green birds, yellow, red, even blue. The woman who would turn out to be Anne Sexton 3 stood behind the bar, the bar to the left, the chairs and tables to the right. Like the chairs and the tables of the barroom, the bar itself seemed made of lumber salvaged from the wreckage of boats. The woman Anne Sexton 3 wore a white dress in the heartbreak cut, her hair white and tall on her head, like a cake. The white of this dress and of the tower of her hair seemed to light the entire place. I judged her as a woman, not unlike the black-haired woman, who half belonged to Time. I judged her as a woman who might keep a book of bad names. I didn't know if she was a witch or not, but I had no doubt that a witch could live on land as well as on a boat, maybe even in a tree. Though a crowd rustled outside and a storm seemed in the offing, there weren't many people in the Oligarchy, the long swoop of the bar itself, stairs leading up to an open hallway where the sun ones and the moons ones bustled, readying themselves for the night. I stood in the doorway with my meteor eye adjusting to the light. Deep in the place sat a kid, about my age, with green hair, he wearing the pink shorts that marked him as an earner. The green-haired kid just sat there, staring into next year, while two sailors, conferring at a table near a great white piano, spoke in low tones to each other, toying with their costume facial hair. Behind the bar the woman Anne Sexton 3 reached up and cupped the dangling bird nearest her, yellow with its beak half open. She set this bird spinning on its line and she leaned against the bar and spoke to a man with a face that looked a lot like a face, yes, but a face turned inside out. This man curled over the bar across from the woman Anne Sexton 3, seeming to laugh up toward her hair. The two sailors eyed the green-haired kid for a bit, then turned their eyes on me. They pooled turquoise-and-orange coins on the tabletop and gestured at me to come over. Instead, I walked up to the bar, still wet from my swim from the *Veronica* to the docks, and stood before the woman who would turn out to be Anne Sexton 3.

"I'm Orphan Thing," I said to her. "I recently invented the word *love.*"

—

The woman Anne Sexton 3 introduced herself.

"I haven't been writing poetry lately, Orphan Thing," Anne Sexton 3 said. "I blame it on this good mood I've been in."

"I'm glad your mood is good," I said.

She stood in the glow of her own dress-light, puffs of white powder rising gently from her high white hair. There was a clock on the wall above her head. It moved very quickly. It fizzed off its minutes.

"You're Anne Sexton 3," I said. "Who were the other Anne Sextons?"

"No one knows," Anne Sexton 3 said. She said, of the poetry she hadn't been writing, "I've still got a couple old ones memorized, if you'd like to hear one."

"Of course," I said.

Anne Sexton 3 touched a powdered hand to her throat. Her face was visible and round. "This a one-line poem," she said. "The title is 'What the Devil Told Me.' The poem is: 'Fruit is not a sex crime.'"

—

I don't think anyone knows what poetry is supposed to be, really, but there was something I liked about it. It made you feel small and warm. It made you feel like you were a person, on Earth, worth talking to, maybe the only person, maybe because everyone else was dead except you, you and the voice talking to you. I thanked the woman Anne Sexton 3 for these feelings and I walked across the creaky bar floor and up the wooden stairway to the working level of the Oligarchy, the key she'd given me jingling in my hand. From behind each door lining that hallway I heard the flutter of voices, the sun ones and the moon ones talking and laughing expectantly. Before I'd swum from the houseboat *Veronica* to this place, the black-haired woman had given me, for my protection on land, a couple of bang-knives, and I'd put them in the pockets of my knee-length pink shorts, one in each pocket. I wondered if the other sun ones and moon ones carried weapons for protection like I did. I wondered if I was a sun one or a moon one.

—

I keyed into my room and stepped in, small bed with pink sheets and pillowcases, a coatrack, a single easy chair, a small dresser, a rusty showerhead sticking from the back wall, a spirit lamp burning on the nightstand. I crossed the room and stood, looking out the window, the view out onto the docks and walkway below, an outdoor seating area, or more like a park, between the Oligarchy and the docks. Down there in the park, men in groups of twos and threes milled, sat on benches, looking up at the windows of the Oligarchy. I thought these men—trawlermen, boat mechanics, farmers from the surrounding hills—to be men too poor to pay for company. One man in a long overcoat stood smoking a cigarette, looking up at my window and touching the fly of his trousers, which is when I realized I could be seen, standing with the spirit lamp burning behind me. The man in the long coat blew smoke in my direction, upwards at the window. His smoke would reach me if he could not. I looked down at this man as I thought about the black-haired woman, maybe fishing for catfish that night in the bays of the southern end, how long she might be gone while I earned for her in this place. She was a lonely person in some ways and in some ways I think she preferred it. I wanted to do well at the Oligarchy, to make myself useful, necessary. Though at the same time there was this huge world out there, threatening to get larger, Torsion Cove and whatever else, so much beyond what I'd seen of it, and I wanted to keep the world as small as I could, to keep it compressed to a ball I could pass to the black-haired woman, let her put it under her bed along with the book of bad names. There was too much longing, not all of it mine. I removed the two bang-knives from my pockets and turned from the window and hid the knives under the cool pillows of the bed. The black-haired woman had put her money in my father's hand. Now it was time to start paying back a little for the upkeep of my life.

—

The first job to knock on my door wore long chin-whiskers—fake, but well faked—and he held the brim of his doffed hat daintily between two fingers.

"Anne says you're new," the man said. He crossed the room and sat in the easy chair.

"That's right," I said.

He got a look at me. "Anyways," he said, "I've never seen you before."

"That's right," I said.

"I suppose you're telling me," he said, his eyes shifting off, "that I'm your first job."

I sat down on the edge of the bed. "Yes," I said.

"How many fibs can you tell an hour?" he asked.

I didn't answer anything. I wasn't sure what *fib* meant. The man looked around to put his hat somewhere and eventually chose to lay it on the floor. "Hell," he said, "I don't know what I'm complaining about."

"No problem," I said.

"It usually doesn't take me too long, anyway," the man said. He unzipped his pants. "I'm just telling you," he said. "It's a sensitivity thing. It's over before I know it."

"I get it," I said.

I stood from the bed and crossed the room and knelt in front of him.

"It's hardly worth the coin," he said.

"That's all right," I said.

"Please don't talk anymore," he said. "That just makes it worse."

"Okay," I said.

"You better hurry," he said, "it's almost over with already."

—

The second job was an older man with a costume mustache almost the width of his shoulders. He had it propped up off his face with little stilts of toothpick. He had a tattoo on the underside of his right forearm that said, "I could be someone's father."

"It's not like I lay awake at night thinking of a boy," he said.

He sat down on the edge of the bed. He put his hat upside down on his lap and looked into the mouth of it. I sat down next to him.

"What do you think about?" I asked.

"Wilma," he said to the hat.

"I bet Wilma's nice," I said.

"Yes," he said, "except for how she's a bigger whore than you."

"Okay," I said.

"That's not very charitable," the man said. With a careful finger he policed the architecture of his great mustache. He said, "I apologize to you. To you if not to Wilma."

"I'm sure Wilma's very fond of you," I said.

He looked at me sideways, a flash of wariness in his eyes. "I'm not taking my clothes all the way off, if that's what you're after," he said.

—

You looked a little bit at the carriage of their many hats, you tried to learn from their tattoos, but mainly what you did is you looked up or down or over your shoulder and you focused on the facial hair. I found the complication of their many beards intriguing. It seemed a different world, these false beards and waves and filigrees, a world of care and practice. The men worried over their facial hair like they might over children. I wondered what it might be like to be such a man, if that were even a possibility for me. There were so many different styles of facial hair, different tones and support systems. Though the third job, when he came into the room, he had gone about it a different way. He didn't wear a beard of false hair at all, but had one inked onto his actual face, sharp black mustache and sharper black goatee. It gave him a stern, fastidious, two-dimensional look, like a man stepped from an illustration in a book. This kind of thing was what was so fascinating to me, nor did he wear a hat. He stood slender in the doorway, a vial in his hands, full of what would turn out to be a delicate and perfumed oil. From the rooms on either side of mine, one heard the sounds of the fashion of various lovemakings. You could hear the great white piano, in the barroom below, start up, a song like a clanking of teeth. Without saying anything, the man with the inked-on beard walked past me and crossed the room and knelt at the edge of the bed. I went over and stood next to him, not sure what he wanted. He looked up at me.

"You're very tall," he said.

"Thank you," I said.

"Please sit down," he said.

I sat on the edge of the bed. He looked down at my feet.

"What do I call you?" he asked.

"Veronica."

"Veronica," he said, "you must have had a hard day."

"It's been interesting," I said, as Veronica, whoever Veronica was. Through the wall came the noise of a man barking like he'd been shot.

"Sounds like they're having fun in there," the ink-bearded man said.

"Probably," I said.

"You've had a hard day, Monica, and you must be very tired."

I didn't correct him about my name, since my name wasn't Veronica, nor Monica either. I felt I didn't have the right. "It's been a very hard day," I said.

"Just sit back and relax, Monica." He removed the dropper from the vial and applied a couple of drops of oil to each of the tops of my feet. He smiled up at me to see what I thought about the oil. Then one by one he began massaging my feet.

"Doesn't that feel nice?" he said. He looked up at me from under his lashes. He used a little more oil. His hands were gentle and sure. "These feet are strong and light and they carry you from place to place," he said.

—

After the ink-bearded man left, I showered beneath the rusty spigot and then waited on the edge of the bed for another job to come in. I heard a chiming laugh in the hallway and I stood and opened the door to see a chubby trawlerman walking down the hall toward me.

But on his arm was a tall blond girl in a pink dress—she would turn out to be the laugher—so thin she disappeared from the vision of my meteor eye and I had to shut that eye to see her. Her blond hair was cut severely to box in her face, like the frame of an actual painting. Her knees were clean and sharp and her skin was dark from the sun. She had a flat-footed walk that meant to slap the floor instead of cross it. She was a girl who, with her height and her laughter, would be just as comfortable in daylight as the darkness. She was about my age and she saw me in the doorway and reached out for my hand, passing herself from the man to me.

"Wait here," she said lightly to the man. "I need to talk to my brother."

—

The girl seemed to know me or know who I'd be. She told me her name was Cozilla and around her neck from a pink cord dangled a little silver pocket gun that swung when she turned this way or that. There would be no time in the room, when we were alone in there together, when she didn't touch her body to mine in some way. Though I don't mean that like it sounds, exactly. The touching she did was friendly, sisterly, our thighs pressing together as we walked. A shoulder bump and a side hug. An interlacing of fingers. A clicking together of anklebones. All this in the second it took us to walk from the door to the bed. She caught my elbow with her elbow as we sat down. She crossed her legs so she could get one golden-brown foot in my lap. "I hoped I'd see you here," she said.

"Do I know you?" I said.

"We're best friends," the girl Cozilla said.

—

In the room next to us you could hear the sound of weeping, the sound of a gurgle like breath cut off, a table turning over, a palm slapping the wall.

"I bet that's a real good time," the girl Cozilla said.

"You're not going to shoot me, are you?" I asked, pointing at the gun.

"Not unless you start murdering me," she said. She showed me the pink cord around her neck. She lifted the cord high and she looped it around my neck too, so that the cord encircled both of our necks, like we were both a single animal with two heads and just one jewel to look at, the gun on its pink cord. So we looked down at the little gun together. I touched its handle with my fingertips. "I love that gun to death," the girl Cozilla said. "A black-haired witch gave it to me."

—

"You have a lot of questions but there isn't much time," the girl Cozilla said. There was a breathlessness to her, a way she tilted her chin at you to look at you up from under. She smelled good, lightly cooked. She poked a finger at the door, on the other side of which the chubby trawlerman waited for her, to indicate why there wasn't much time. "I've got a job to do," she said.

"Do you know the black-haired woman?" I asked.

"Of course," she said. "Sometimes I row a little yellow canoe out to the *Veronica*. Sometimes I catch a ride out with trawlermen."

"When's the last time you saw her?"

"I'm not good with times and days," she said.

I wasn't good with times and days either.

"Did you come down from the hills tonight?" I asked, thinking of how I'd watched the sun ones and the moon ones flying to the Oligarchy on their zip lines, assembling on the roof like the petals of a flower reunited, wondering if the girl Cozilla had been among them.

"Yes," she said.

I shook my head in wonder. "It's pretty," I said, "watching them fly down the lines, all in pink like that."

She shook her head yes. "It must be lovely," she said. "I would like to be able to watch it, from afar, myself someday." She stood and we walked hand in hand around the small room for a bit, like we might be going somewhere specific. Then she paused us at the window and we looked down at the sad coinless men in the park. She rubbed her nose with the palm of her hand, giving her fine-featured face—for a second—a bit of a piglike look. I liked her a lot. She was easy to talk to and she had different ways of moving and being than I was used to. She poked her face out through the serious frame of her hair. "It's nice coming down the zip lines," she said thoughtfully. "That's for sure. The wind blowing all around you. You feel light and free. You feel like you could let go and just flap off to the moon. The harder part," she said, "is climbing back up the hill, come morning, when you're all worn out from the night and your legs feel so heavy."

"I hadn't thought of that," I said.

She pointed at my reflection in the window.

"I like your meteor eye," she said.

—

"I wanted to give you something, Orphan Thing," she said.

It was weird to hear this name come from someone other than the black-haired woman, but I supposed it was how names worked. They got around. The girl Cozilla had her arm around my waist and she planted one of her feet on top of my foot. Once she had the foot in place on top of mine, she removed her arm from my waist and started searching the pockets of her pink dress. It was like she was afraid she might lose you, or that she would get lost herself, so she always tried to keep a hand or a foot or a knee in contact. Her left hand came out of the pink dress with a little coin purse in it. I recognized it as a purse, of course, because of the Great Pornography I'd seen on the houseboat *Veronica*. This was just a very small one though, utilitarian. It was leather and pink. She handed it to me. She hooked my elbow with her elbow and only then did she lift her foot from my foot. I unsnapped the purse and looked into it—empty—then back up at the girl Cozilla.

"You're to keep your coins in it," she said.

"Thank you," I said.

LETTER IN THE BLACK-HAIRED WOMAN'S HAND

—

Dear Orphan Thing,

The alphabet is finally here, but I bet it turns out it's just a blip, billions of years before it, billions of years after it. I know you like my penmanship, so I write this letter. You're in Torsion Cove, kneeling for men with ridiculous facial hair. Thank you.

Here, on the houseboat *Veronica*, I'm fishing for trout off the Sentient Weedbeds. It's the little trout that are good for eating. Therefore I've sized down for them with nubbins of corn, the smallest of barbless hooks, a strong but sensitive leader I've braided from strands of my own hair. I like to think of those little trout. I like to think of their little teeth and little hearts.

I don't like to write too much about it because I get sentimental, but I've been thinking about murdering you a lot lately. There are ideas loose on the houseboat *Veronica*. In every corner of every room I can see your body slumped over, breathing its last. I know you'd like me to talk more about it, to hear what's going on in my mind. And I know what it's like to want to be close to someone's thoughts. When you kneel on the deck and look up at me as I lift the heartbreak-cut green dress, I know I am going to be close to the literal contents of your skull. I would like to place my heartbeat in the center of your brain, to feel the neurons firing signals back and forth through me.

Not that I want to crack open your skull, either, nor spoon the contents of it to myself. Excuse these thoughts, as they are a witch's thoughts, a witch's transitions, though I hardly know what the word *witch* means anymore. The problem of being a human, I suppose, isn't that the human being will die, but that they can only die the one time. The fact of my serious regard for you makes itself known to me not in the way that I feel I want you to live forever, but that I wish you could die over and over again.

I'm not talking about reincarnation, which you may not have heard about anyway. I mean I want you to die over and over again, in this life, impossible. Yet the one murder will never be quite enough, and so I put it off. And even if I were, tonight, granted a wish, and used that wish to make the body of Orphan Thing immortal, we'd then only arrive on the other side of the problem, which is that once a body is immortal, no one cares that much to murder it. It's a difficult situation your body has put us both in. I know you will do your best with it. With it, I know you are doing your best right now, in Torsion Cove, and I send my regards to you there.

Yours, and in this manner specifically,

The Black-Haired Woman

LONG NIGHT IN TORSION COVE

—

From the dooryway I watched the girl Cozilla and the chubby trawlerman (winking, red faced and big cheeked, tipping his hat to me) walk off down the hall, then turn into one of the rooms together. The girl Cozilla had called me her brother. That word all by itself, working through me like warm water, made me angry with the chubby trawlerman, his smile and the bustiness of his cheeks. I didn't want to see her turn into the room with him, alone in her pink dress and her brown feet spanking the wooden floor. For obvious reasons—tiptoe, charm, and knife—I rarely felt the need to protect the black-haired woman. The girl Cozilla seemed different. Not that she needed protecting, just that I wanted to protect her. She was taller and less organized as a body. Her angles did not seem conversant with each other until they came into contact with the angles of other bodies. I liked to be her brother and I knew I would see this girl Cozilla again. It was a feeling of certainty, and I began wondering if I shouldn't find some gift to give to her when I next saw her, to pay her back, in kindness, for the coin purse. She had not at all needed to give me a gift, but she had. The more time I spent in the world the more kindness I found in it. I stood in the doorway, looking out into the now empty hall, thinking what kind of present a girl like Cozilla might like.

—

I shut the door behind me, walked toward the stairway that led me back down to the barroom. I thought I might want to hear the woman Anne Sexton 3 say another poem from memory. Some people who were there in the barroom before were gone and then some other people had arrived. I saw a different boy in pink shorts, sitting at a back table, this boy with dark shoulder-length hair and bronze skin. He rolled his eyes at me as I came down the stairs, then went back to reading, to himself, from a pamphlet outlining the treatment of venereal woe. There were only a couple other men in the place, really, a farmer with plastic teeth staring into a cup of benzene like he might read the future there, a man who wore a hat that looked like a bird's nest. I sat on the same barstool I'd sat on before. The woman Anne Sexton 3 materialized from a cloud of white powder and set a small jarlet of benzene in front of me.

"You're tall," she said.

"Thank you," I said.

"Your eyes are very far apart," Anne Sexton 3 said. "I think if I stood very close to you, right in front of you, and you only looked directly forward, you wouldn't be able to see me at all."

—

And so the woman Anne Sexton 3 said: "I knew the black-haired woman."

"It seems like I keep meeting people like that," I said, thinking of the girl Cozilla.

"A lot of people know her," said Anne Sexton 3. "The black-haired woman has been around a long time."

"I like that about her."

"Then you like that about me too," she said.

"I guess I do," I said.

She surprised me with a laugh that shook her wig and her wig shot up little geysers of white powder. She said, "I wrote a little poem about the black-haired woman, if you'd care to hear it."

"I'd like that," I said.

"It's a one-line poem," the woman Anne Sexton 3 said. She took my hand in her two hands, tiny globes of white powder balanced on the tips of her eyelashes. She said, "The title of this poem is 'Love in the Time of One Moon and One Sky.' The poem is: 'Things got weird after the insemination.'"

—

A hard wind blew in from the hills and the tin walls of the Oligarchy rattled. The insemination poem made me feel small and warm, a little sleepy. Lashings of rain started up like someone outside pegging handfuls of rice at the building. I admit it felt nice to be indoors, on a steady floor for once, without the totter of the lake upsetting it, as it was on the houseboat *Veronica*, as the houseboat *Veronica* was founded on water, not on land. It felt good to not have to worry about my balance, where my feet should be all the time. The old man with the inside out face turned out to be the player of the great white piano. And just now he came down from the upstairs sex rooms, adjusting himself carnally on the wooden stairs, then sat before the great white piano, now an air about him of elegance, even with the ugliness of his face. The song he sang was of a dead lover, very dear to him. I sat and sipped benzene and smelled the woman Anne Sexton 3's white body powder and listened to the old man's song. It felt good to be a part of this place, though at the same time, again, the world continued to open up in ways I didn't quite trust. Just a short time before I had only really known one person, the black-haired woman. Now, counting Anne Sexton 3 and the girl Cozilla, I knew three times as many. I felt like I stood at the mouth of a cave, looking out on a meadow. The piano man's teeth weren't good teeth, some of them lost to either the Living Dots or to violence or neglect, but he sang around the remainders interestingly, his voice keening from a ditch. Judging by what I made out of the lyrics, the dead lover of the piano man's song had been a good lover. When she'd been alive the lover had wine in her bones and a gravity in her heart. But now it was too bad because the dead lover had been seen cheating on the piano man with worms, nor could her ghost ever be trusted to show up on time.

—

I climbed back up the steps to the upper rooms, thinking of the time the black-haired woman smashed the translucent green worm on my chest, hoping I'd maybe run into the girl Cozilla, but I wouldn't see her again in that place. In the darkness of my room I stood at the single window and looked down into the park between the Oligarchy and the docks of Torsion Cove, feeling melancholy over the old man's song, over the poems of the woman Anne Sexton 3, feeling how old this world was and how briefly I'd been in it. I thought of what the girl Cozilla had said about flying down, in pink, on the zip lines, first the freedom, then the long walk back up the hill at dawn, that heaviness in the planet which you also felt in the center of your body. I felt like one of her, one of them, one of the weary. Through the dark of the trees and bent over rain-slick benches, in the park below my window, I could see the angled bodies of men, coupling and touching, no longer content to look up at the windows of the Oligarchy. Some of the men held up burning candles while they kissed, so that others and I could see them. The men hugged each other to their fanciful beards and they hugged the trees and the branches shook until it almost looked like the trees themselves were seeking solace with each other. Rain fell softly now into the park in thinning silver and I could hear weeping down there too, as if the men had waited for the cover of rain to release their tears. I thought of the black-haired woman, how that night of my vision she'd stood on the deck of the houseboat *Veronica* without the business of her clothes, in front of the men imprisoned in the geometric towers of the Penal Archipelago, one of them her son, now dead. Why not be a little bit like her? I didn't think it would be presumptuous. I turned on the spirit lamp and removed my pink knee-length shorts. I stood close to the window and I let these men look up at my unclothed body while they worked together in the trees. It was the least I could do. It felt very brave to stand that way. Two men together on a park bench waved up, happy to be accompanied. A man in a bush, alone with himself as far as I could see, hoorahed and blew me a kiss. Another lone man, the same man in the long coat who had looked up at me before, stepped out from the dark edge of the park and stood on the stone walk beneath my window, close enough I could see his eyes. I smiled at him and waved. He lifted his hand, I thought, to wave back, but instead he drew a little X in the air, crossing me out.

—

Of the jobs to follow that night I remembered less the men who wanted the usual contact with my body, remembered more the men who wanted sad or unusual things. One man, for example, who spent his time watching me shower, urging me to be thorough, then after he was satisfied I was clean enough, he simply turned around and left the room. Then one man who just wanted to watch me do push-ups. One man who wanted to spoon with me on the inside and one man who wanted to spoon with me on the outside. One man—he was captain of a shrimp trawler, though not the *Harm and Foam*—who wanted to talk with me about his calling with the shrimp, the currents of water and the mating habits and the oxygenation and the eventual price per pound. Two brothers who asked me to play their third brother, who was dead. One man who exhorted me to shame him for being in love with me. One man who wished for me to enter him instead of the other way around, but I couldn't do this for him.

"You can't do that for me?" he asked.

"I belong to a witch," I said.

"Everyone wants to belong to a witch," he said.

"I'm serious," I said.

"You're the one way," he said, "but not the other?"

"That's right," I said.

"You're the tree and not the flying thing," he said.

"That's how I was told," I said.

"This is a rule?" he said.

"Yes," I said.

He thought a little. "I don't know about this."

"You can get your money back," I said.

"But I think you're not awful to look at," he said.

"Thank you," I said.

Almost to himself he said, "Maybe the mouth."

"Okay."

"And could your name be Terrence?" he asked.

"My name *is* Terrence," I said.

—

Later that night, while I showered again, I heard a knock at my rented door. I wrapped the towel around me and crossed the room, hoping it would be the girl Cozilla, so I could talk to her again, maybe find out, on the sly, what kind of a gift might delight her. But it was not the girl Cozilla, it was the man with the inked-on mustache and goatee, from before, come back again. He'd brought along his vial of oil with him. By this time my body was truly tired out and I have to say I was happy to see him.

"I hope you can forgive me," he said.

"For what?" I asked.

"I realized my mistake. When I saw you last," he said, "I called you Monica, not Veronica."

"That's okay," I said.

"It's not okay, Veronica," he said, "but you're very kind to say so."

—

Veronica again, I stood aside for the man and turned to hang the pink towel on the coatrack. When I turned back, the man already knelt bedside, waiting for me. I sat down on the edge of the bed and I lifted a foot for him.

"This oil comes all the way from the domed island cities of the East," he said.

"I've never been to those cities," I said.

"Shall I tell you about them?"

I thought about it. "No," I said. "I want to keep the world the way it is right now."

"Nice and small and well-behaved," he said.

"Yes," I said.

"Well," he said, "it's a very fine oil anyway."

"It seems very fine."

He said, rubbing the oil onto his palms, "You must have had a busy night, Veronica."

"And may I ask your name?" I asked.

"Elwood," he said.

"Elwood," I said, "let me tell you all about it."

A LITTLE UNCLEAR WHAT THE MOON LOOKED LIKE

—

Close of business, daylight nursing in. With bang-knives in both pockets and the coin purse in my hand, I walked the wooden walkway from the Oligarchy and down the slight hill toward the gap-toothed docks, through and around the now-empty sex park, the coin purse full of the coin I'd earned for the black-haired woman. I could see the light of the moon but not the moon. When the woman Anne Sexton 3 had paid me out the black-haired woman's percentage of the earnings, she also relayed the message of how the black-haired woman lay at anchor in the mouth of Torsion Cove, expecting my return that very night. A little bird had told her this, Anne Sexton 3 had said, reaching up to cup a dangling taxidermied bird in the palm of her hand. I was to swim out to the black-haired woman with the coin. I was happy that I wouldn't have to be away from the black-haired woman for more than the one night. I would return to her feeling like a human being who had had some effect on the world. It was a nice thing to work at a job. You felt sharper, more visible, ratified. Even the trees wanted to know you better. The moonlight yet held the sun back from the sky and the walkway shone silver with the earlier rain. I still wore the slickness of the ink-bearded man's foot-oil on my feet, which made the going a little treacherous. I touched at the wooden handrail and I heard no voices coming from the docks ahead of me, nor from the Oligarchy behind. The little settlement seemed fast asleep, its citizenry tamped down by love and drink, its pink-clad sun ones and moon ones trudging unseen, now, back up into the hills for their rest. With the coin I'd earned—I imagined this as I walked—the black-haired woman could buy gasoline and the little sachets of the living tobacco that she favored. She could buy hair ties for her immense hair. She could make repairs to the houseboat *Veronica* and maybe she'd buy a bolt of cloth with which to make new heartbreak-cut green dresses.

—

Coming up the walkway toward me, now, was the man in the long thin coat, eyes slotted, his form pulsing silver in warning. Either demon or ghost, said the meteor eye. This was the man who'd crossed me with an X in the park as if to mark his spot for later. Now I knew what he literally meant by that. Now he had a claw hammer in his hand and it made the shadow of his right arm thin and gangly, like a puppet's. He moved up the walkway, jerkily, quickly, as if he had more legs than two.

—

As he came I stopped on the walkway and stepped back.

"Too late," the man said. He swung the hammer and I slipped from the rain and the oil on my feet and I fell and instead of my head the claw of the hammer chunked into the handrail of the walkway. "You lucky thing," the man said. Below him I fought to get the bang-knife from my right pocket. Close to me the smell of the man's body belled out mousy and rotten. His boots looked cracked and fed upon. His eyes seemed forlorn, like he was already grieving me.

—

In my fumble for the bang-knife I must have pressed the go button three times, not meaning to. My right pocket burst and I felt the blade shoot, outside in, through my thigh, then worse than the thigh. I collapsed to the right from the pain between my legs as the man's hammer looped by again. I curled up and vomited onto the toes of the man's boots.

"This is an embarrassment," the man said.

—

The man kicked vomit from his boots like he was doing a little dance and he worked at the hammer to free it from the wooden rail. This murder was disappointing him. I didn't like to think the man might murder me at all, which would mean that I'd not live to be murdered on the houseboat *Veronica*, which was how I'd been imagining the future wanted it. I didn't like the idea of walking through the invisible wall with this dumb story of a hammer to tell to the dead ones. I figured the dead hadn't heard of such a togetherness as the murder I preferred speak to them of, once it came time to speak to them, not this one and its hammer, but the one at the black-haired woman's hands. That was a story you would be proud to tell the dead. And once you were dead you'd want to turn around, look back where you'd come from, and tell it to the living, too. Sometimes the murder you want is the murder that keeps you alive, or this was the thought that got me past the sight of the cauliflower of blood welling from the crotch of my shorts, the fear I might've neutered myself with the bang-knife. I pushed myself upright and asked my would-be killer if he could wait for just a second.

—

"Why wait?"

I lifted the coin purse. "Take it," I said.

"This isn't a robbery," he said. "This is a sex murder." He knocked the coin purse from my hand like it was a dirty thing he didn't want coming between us. He raised the hammer a third time and I reached up with my left hand, which had the second bang-knife in it. No one thinks you'd have one bang-knife, let alone two. They don't make them anymore. I touched the business end to his sternum and fired it, like the black-haired woman taught me. The claw hammer dropped from the man's hand and thunked between my feet and the man made a face like someone had opened an umbrella inside him.

SEWN UP, FOR A SECOND TIME, ON THE HOUSEBOAT *VERONICA*

—

"What'd you think of the moon?" the black-haired woman asked, scooting closer to me on the green sewing stool. Bleeding between the legs, I'd swum from the docks of Torsion Cove to the houseboat *Veronica* with the heavy coin purse between my teeth and the slot-eyed man's claw hammer tucked into my shorts. Now I took the black-haired woman's question about the moon while laying face up and breathing on the foredeck. I took her question about the moon as kindness. Last night's moon had been one we'd not seen together, unlike other moons I could name. She wanted to lay a path between our heads, I thought, so this lost moon didn't separate us. Though maybe this was too much information to be getting from a single question about the moon. I'd lost a lot of blood, no doubt, and feared weakly for my testicles. I hadn't been able to look between my legs at the horror I'd see there. Furthermore it turned out the girl Cozilla now stood on the stern deck, too, peeping over the black-haired woman's shoulder, looking comfortable and like she belonged, her eyes curious upon me, now wearing not the pink dress but a yellow one in the bell tower cut that made her skin glow gold, her neck like a stalk grown out from the dense sun of the black-haired woman's hair. It felt strange to have a third person on the houseboat *Veronica* again, to be bleeding in front of two people. Neither did I remember many or any times where I'd needed to speak to two women at once.

But I was navigating new feelings anyway. My murder of the man in the long coat had left in me a fierce pang, like anything you could name was supposed to be inside me. Whatever I had wanted before, I wanted more of it now. I looked up at these two women, the black-haired woman and the girl Cozilla, one blond and one dark of hair, the shallow tank of the sky above them.

—

The girl Cozilla kept one hand on the black-haired woman's shoulder while the houseboat *Veronica* skipped over the Sentient Weedbeds and the black-haired woman cut away the pink shorts from my body. Something gnawed uncomfortably at my back, pressed between me and the brazier foredecking, which I realized was the dead man's claw hammer. I was laying on it. It had been my plan to give the claw hammer to the girl Cozilla, as a gift. It didn't seem the right time to be giving a gift just then, not when one of the three of us was bleeding. I raised my back and reached beneath and handed the hammer to the black-haired woman. She laid it on the deck at her feet and I closed my eyes and readied myself for her stitches.

"It's kind of a mess down there," the girl Cozilla said, over the black-haired woman's shoulder, her voice not stricken or worried but interested. Yet I wasn't listening to her. Primarily now I was listening to the Sentient Weedbeds cruising beneath us. It was hard not to listen to the weeds in this part of the lake. They spoke to you. You could feel the sentient weeds shooting up their vegetable fantasy into your mind, taking on your thought. The weedbed fanned twenty miles long and it wanted you to join it. The weedbed wanted you down beneath to tell it all the news of the dry world. It sang of all the many bodies it had known.

—

Against the bounce of the boat, the black-haired woman pulled a strand of hair from her head and held it to the eye of the needle, threading it through.

"What did you think of the moon, Orphan Thing?" the girl Cozilla reminded me.

"I couldn't get a sense of it," I answered.

The black-haired woman agreed. She shooed the vampire moths of her hair from the wounds between my legs, their whitish pink wings dull in the dawn light. The girl Cozilla set a spirit lamp on the deck beside me to give the black-haired woman more light to work by. The pink moths ran sorties from the black-haired woman's hair, down to the lure of the spirit lamp and back. "The moon was tricky all night long," the black-haired woman said. "At first I thought it looked a little like a snail with horns." She splashed benzene on the needle and between my legs. "Then an eagle's eye. Then a shell half-buried on the beach. Then an unplugged hole. Then I didn't know where it was." She lowered her head over my body and the girl Cozilla leaned to look too. I noted a similarity in the triangular shape of both women's faces. They looked like long-lost sisters, gold and black. I felt I was the newcomer to the boat, not the girl Cozilla, which feeling also made the black-haired woman a little strange to me. I felt like I'd stumbled foreign onto some special habitat. I looked around to make sure the boat I was on was the boat I remembered. At the edge of the lamplight, there, I saw two little pinprick eyeflashes, one of the toads from the garden on the balcony deck, come down to the fore-deck, hunting for the pink moths of the black-haired woman's hair. I watched the toad squeeze its eyes closed to swallow a trembling pink wing.

"There are," the black-haired woman said, sending the needle quickening through me, "scorch marks on the upper right thigh, there and there. You'll be bruised from the concussion, it looks, from the midthigh up past the hip. The blade fired clean through the muscle of the outer thigh and came out the inside, on a slant, puncturing the purse of the scrotum." She looked rightward at the girl Cozilla, there just hanging off her shoulder. "Can you see?" she asked the girl.

"I can see," the girl Cozilla said.

The black-haired woman stopped sewing and she moved me around down there, up and down, left and right, then wiped at me with a rag already bloody. "It's not as bad as it looks at first. He was lucky," she said to the girl. "I don't think anything is ruined. There's a nick in the testicular wall, just a little one." She turned to look at the girl Cozilla again. "Can you see?" she asked the girl.

"I can see," the girl Cozilla said.

—

The houseboat *Veronica* ran north toward the greenish glow of the Penal Archipelago, over the densest of the Sentient Weedbeds, the purple and yellow waterflowers so thick they read as the roof of a house more than surface of a lake, startled fish arcing across the nose of the boat in the morning mist. The sentient weeds whispered how I could have gills if I wanted them bad enough. I sat up from the deck and I looked down between my legs at the black-haired woman's handiwork, three tight black seams, one on each side of my thigh, the third smaller in length but denser in stitch, there on the right inside hang of the scrotum. It was like her penmanship, but different.

"Thank you," I said to the black-haired woman.

"Don't mention it," she said.

"It was a really long night," I said.

"It was a *really* long night," the girl Cozilla said. She kept one hand on the black-haired woman's shoulder—she was much taller than the black-haired woman—and she came around to sit down on the deck at my feet, between me and the black-haired woman, the girl making sure to touch her toes to the tips of my toes, at the same time leaning her back against the black-haired woman's knees, in contact with both of us.

I looked from one woman's face to the other. I took my time. "I feel very lucky that we're all here," I said, "on the foredeck of the houseboat *Veronica*."

—

The black-haired woman counted the orange-and-turquoise coins in the pink coin purse I'd given her and she scooted her stool close to me and lifted her heartbreak-cut green dress. Cozilla stood up and sat beside me. The money I'd made belonged to a witch and I knelt with the throb between my legs and the girl Cozilla held my hand. The black-haired woman looped one candle leg around my neck and drew me close to her in the crook of it. I opened my mouth for her and she said: "Not a man or a woman in shoes or in bare feet. Not a man or a woman with a headache or a man or a woman passed out or a man or a woman standing in a doorway at night. Not a man or a woman who likes a necklace and not a man or a woman whose favorite color is blue and not a man or a woman who has given birth. Not a man or a woman who breathes and not a man or a woman who is dead. Not a man or a woman with paint on their toenails and not a man or a woman who likes to think about mathematics. Not a man or a woman who lives in a tower and not a man or a woman who has written a very good book and not a man or a woman who has read that book."

—

You out there in the interesting future: the boat runs one way, the sun runs the other. And which way was forward? And who stitches you when you need stitching? I didn't know. I don't know what you know either, nor what it must be like for you, alive still, going on and on, still far from the stepping-off point. And meanwhile, no matter what the map wants, no matter which way the boat is going, you stand, you turn, you walk whichever way you want to walk.

—

The black-haired woman drew her pink chevrons on my cheekbones and then she hustled the houseboat *Veronica* North until the sun made off with our shadow and we cleared the Sentient Weedbeds. She anchored the houseboat *Veronica* off a rock point just shy of the Knee Keys. Saying she needed to sleep it off, she retired to her quarters and left the girl Cozilla and I sitting together, arm in arm, on the foredeck. Now the girl Cozilla wore a yellow sun hat to match her bell tower-cut dress and there was no time on the foredeck when she didn't touch her body to mine in some way.

"I thought your stitches looked nice," the girl Cozilla said.

"Thank you," I said.

"I have the Living Dots. Do you?"

"Yes," I said. I pointed out a couple of scars on my thigh. "The black-haired woman gave them to me."

"Of course," she said.

"Was she the one who gave you yours?" I asked.

"No," the girl Cozilla said. "I wish," she said.

—

"Do you know the man, Elwood, who carries a vial of fine eastern oil with him?" I asked.

"Yes," she said. "Elwood's one of my favorites."

I nodded. I thought about the name Elwood, which sounded made up. I asked: "How many people do you know by name?"

"Hundreds," Cozilla said. She said, "Way too many."

I smelled the girl's skin cooking in the sun and I felt hungry and I thought about the world the girl Cozilla knew, thick with people who could fit into a hundred names. She was an interesting person. She had that breathless way of talking but she didn't seem to spook. She wore more than one kind of dress. I remembered how when I first met her, too, she wore a pocket gun on a pink cord around her neck, but she wasn't wearing it anymore. I decided I liked her as much armed as I did unarmed. She put a hand on my shoulder, used it to push herself up from the deck. She kept her palm on the top of my head and she walked around me to sit on the other side.

"You sure like touching people," I said.

"It reminds me how I'm on a planet," she said.

THE GIVING OF A GIFT

—

We sat there in the sun, looking out at the lake, the girl Cozilla and I. We counted (as they passed us by, this way and that) a couple of trawlerboats, a bloodboat, a personal yacht with a shining silver sail.

"I want to give you a gift," I said to the girl Cozilla. With her hooked onto my elbow like she was, I had to lean over to get the claw hammer, there shining in the sun beneath the green sewing stool, me half dragging the girl Cozilla to get to it. It was why I'd brought the hammer from Torsion Cove, to give it to this girl who'd been so kind as to give me, a stranger, a coin purse made of leather. The hammer was the only idea I'd had, giftwise, but I thought it a good idea. The hammer gleamed ugly in the sun and the wooden handle looked gnawed on, but I hoped the girl would like it. It had failed to murder me. It was a special hammer.

"This," I said, "is a hammer."

I handed it to her. We both looked at it.

"I've never been given a hammer before," she said.

"It's a lucky hammer," I said.

She held it in her hands, testing the weight. "It *is* lucky," she decided.

She laid the hammer gently on the deck and looked down at it, as if the luck of the hammer might better be glimpsed that way. The metal of it drew a miniature version of the sun into its gleam. "I'll always treasure this beautiful hammer," the girl said.

—

Behind us through the galley we could hear the sound of the black-haired woman showering. The girl Cozilla made a bridge of the hammer by resting its metal head on my left foot and the handle on her right foot. As we sat there looking at the hammer connecting us, an automated vending boat nosed around a point just up-lake and crawled white and blocky down the shore toward us. Its robot program told it where the houseboat *Veronica* was. Its robot program anchored it off the houseboat *Veronica*, just a short swim away. It idled there at its polite distance in case anyone on board the *Veronica* would want to buy something.

"Shall we swim over to it?" the girl Cozilla asked.

"I gave all my coin to the black-haired woman."

"I'm buying," she said.

—

The enclosed business area of the vending boat was tightly air-conditioned, so cold in that small space that it made the small space even smaller. Along the interior walls loomed a dozen or so dented machines the size of refrigerators. Our clothes were wet from the swim and the air-conditioning ran cold and bright against us. The girl Cozilla shivered and wrung her fine blond frame of hair and there was no one on the boat at all. It was a robot boat. It didn't smell much like anything. We walked the line of machines hand in hand, looking in through the glass at the items on display in each. There was a machine full of fancy underwear that I didn't look at too closely. There was a machine stocked with pamphlets of lake literature and folklore, a machine selling packets of seeds for vegetables and flowers, a machine shining with fishhooks and lures and shrink-wrapped bags of chub minnows and dried shrimp, one machine filled with makeup and accessories, bullet-looking lipsticks and eye pencils and false eyelashes. The girl Cozilla dropped a couple of coins into the slot of this machine and pulled the lever that promised her a packet of shiny body decals. They thunked into the cradle. We walked down and around the machines, looking in each, looking at each other's faces in the reflection of the glass. The girl Cozilla paused before a machine glowing with psychedelic pink-and-green light and she fed it a couple of orange-and-turquoise coins. She pulled a lever that dropped a sachet of the living tobacco the black-haired woman favored. The girl Cozilla was very thoughtful of others. She hooked her finger into the belt loop of my pink shorts and she let me tow her along.

"Get whatever you like," she said.

—

Finally I bought box of grape candies I thought I could share with the girl Cozilla. The girl Cozilla and I stood on the exit deck of the vending boat, back in the warm focus of the sun. We stood there chewing the grape candy, looking at each other. I didn't know what grapes tasted like, but if they tasted anything like the candy, then I was all for them. The girl smiled to taste the candy, too, and I saw how her tongue had gone purple behind her teeth. She punched me in the shoulder.

"It's so good I want to die," she said.

—

The girl tore the plastic off the packet of body decals. They were like a little book and she opened it.

"Do you want me to pick one for you?" she said.

"Yes," I said.

"Not the dolphin," she said, looking into the packet. "Not the octopus. Not the moon. Here," she said. We leaned against the deck railing together. She unpeeled a decal from the packet and lay it sticky side up on her palm. She pressed her palm to my chest and when she took her hand away there was a little silver heart there.

"A second heart to wear over the first," she said.

—

The wounds between my legs started to ache and the girl Cozilla fixed the decal of the dolphin on the inside of her left ankle. We sat down for a little on the guest chairs lined up on the exit deck of the vending boat. We looked out and over at the houseboat *Veronica*, nestled against the green shore.

"I wonder what her dreams are like," the girl Cozilla said aloud. I knew she was talking about the black-haired woman. I had my feet crossed at the ankles and the girl crossed her feet and lifted them and laid them down across my ankles. That way our bodies formed a V. The sun pushed down on us testingly.

"Sometimes I hear her making noises in her sleep," I said.

"Me too," she said.

We nodded our heads and watched the *Veronica* dip and shudder in the small waves. I helped myself to another of the grape candies, but by this time the sun had started its drop and the sweetness of the candy made me a little sick. I could feel how highly the girl Cozilla regarded the black-haired woman and this made me like the girl all the more, but there was more to it than that. She'd called me her brother and I wanted to be her brother. And when I was thinking about the word *brother* she asked me:

"Did you have any brothers or sisters?"

I shook my head. I thought of the boy who looked like me and smelled like me. "It's not clear if I did or not," I said. "How about you?"

"Sisters," she said. "Most of them were no good, including me. But I liked my sister Lemma."

—

"When did you realize there was another world?" she asked.

Alone with her on the vending boat I told the story of the black-haired woman's penmanship, that other world, how it vibrated, how it seemed to belong not on the page, but elsewhere, higher, floating up to whatever thing it was that pressed its face against the sky, looking in and down at us. I thought there could be another world up there, you know, off to wherever the penmanship floated. The girl Cozilla agreed that the black-haired woman's penmanship was considerable. Then, in the spirit of fairness, she told me the story of when she, herself, first realized there was another world.

"My sister Lemma had a purse. It was a huge purse. It had secret inner compartments. It was black with silver snaps and zippers. Lemma was very proud of it. She was my big sister." The girl

Cozilla thought for a bit. She lifted her ankles from my ankles and bent over and picked up my left foot and held it like it was a small animal. "I loved Lemma's purse more than anyone should love a purse, that much I will say. I'd lay there at night and think about that purse. I'd think about dumping out the contents. I'd think about organizing the contents. And I'd think about all of the things I'd keep in a purse when I grew up. And my sister Lemma was gorgeous. I'm okay, but Lemma, when she was fourteen, my god. My father said how when Lemma walked, the trees just burst into flames. He wasn't much of a father, saying things like that, but he wasn't wrong. I'd look at Lemma holding that purse and I'd want to cry. I wanted to be Lemma, or, at the very least, to climb into the purse and have Lemma carry me around in it. There was all this pretty stuff inside it. Candy and special pills and hair ties. Lipstick and mascara. Loose earrings. Her smokes and her dream book. She kept love letters in that purse, on the secret. Knives and maps. Whole tomatoes. And my sister Lemma was very nice about the purse, she wouldn't brag or hog. She let me carry the purse sometimes. Or she'd even lend me a compartment, one of the side zippers, just for me. She'd sit on the floor and she'd empty out the compartment that was going to be mine. And then she'd let me put all my little stuff in it. She'd let me carry her purse back and forth across the room, like I was going somewhere a lady might go. You could fit the world inside that purse and at the same time it rode the shoulder so lightly."

BLOOD ON THE DANCE FLOOR

—

Sometime later that night I sat with the black-haired woman on the aft deck, where she had herself rigged for catfish, the houseboat *Veronica* having run complete the length of the lake and now resting at anchor in the mouth of the bay of Port Sisterfield. From that position, over the aft rail, we had the view of the lake's biggest city, lit up pink by the two great lighthouses flanking each side of the bay. The city of Port Sisterfield was a different thing than the settlement of Torsion Cove, more metal than wood, more fire than mud. Some of its central buildings ran as tall, taller even, than the lighthouses on either side of the bay, tall as the hills trying to loom up behind on the smudged horizon. There were too many buildings to point out singly and they seemed to clutch together anyway and you could hear, even that far out in Crescent Lake, the total sound of it, the grind and the hum, the roar of many voices cheering in unison, the cry of metal swaying in the light wind, unknown alarms and beeps, the pitch of small engines, all the city bright and circuited, like the inside of an alien piece of fruit. The city seemed alive even without considering all the people who no doubt lived there and moved through it. It was very hard to imagine being there, walking on its streets, moving in and out of its buildings. The black-haired woman scooted her chair closer to mine and rested her great head of hair on my shoulder.

"Sometimes it looks so nice from a distance," the black-haired woman said. "It almost makes me wish I still set foot on land."

—

Just a short time before this, though, I'd awakened in my old bed down in the belly hold, the girl Cozilla sleeping sisterly next to me and the ache of my stitched wounds throbbing not unkindly. It felt good to feel your body make its careful little comeback. That afternoon the girl and I'd swum together, hand in hand, from the vending boat, swum as if one person back to the houseboat *Veronica*. We'd not wanted to disturb the black-haired woman, who we knew to be well showered and sleeping it off in her sleeping quarters. My body ached strangely from its use in Torsion Cove, all the positions and upendings, one deltoid but not the other, the tops of my feet sore, a cricket-like chirp in the spine, and I supposed it was the same with the girl Cozilla. We walked tiredly into the enclosed galley level and down the ladderway silently, to the belly hold, I with my silver decal heart covering the true heart, she with the silver dolphin on the ankle. We lay there in the one small bed and we talked together of the black-haired woman.

"Does she ask you to stand up so she can describe you?" I asked.

The girl Cozilla shook her head no. We turned on our separate pillows so we were looking at each other. The girl asked, "Does she rub the small of your back to help you get to sleep?"

"Yes," I said, though this was a lie. I don't remember the black-haired woman ever doing anything like that. I asked, "When you close your eyes, can you picture the black-haired woman's face?"

The girl Cozilla closed her eyes. I closed mine. Together we tried to picture the black-haired woman's face. I, of course, could not. I never could. I could see the hair, the pinpoints of the eyes, the slash of the chin, but little else.

"I can see her face," the girl Cozilla said, "just like she was laying here between us. There is a kindness in her eyes," she said, "there is a white glow to the skin, there is a defiance to the mouth, there are exactly sixty-eight teeth."

We opened our eyes and looked at each other. It made me feel bad that I couldn't remember the black-haired woman's face like the girl Cozilla could. But I didn't let on. I asked, "And does she talk about knives?"

"Not really," the girl said. "I see the knives, though. I know they're around."

"Yes," I said, "they're all around."

She shut her eyes again.

"I don't usually like to be in a room with a knife," the girl Cozilla said, "but I'm trying to learn better habits."

—

Then we'd wished each other a good sleep and drifted off hand in hand. There would be no other way to sleep next to her but hand in hand. There would be no way for her not to be touching you. I wondered if the girl dreamed, and if she did dream, did she dream of a baby she might make with the black-haired woman. The thought slotted a little iron bar through my chest, which made me know the thought was probably correct, a baby, in or out of a dream. Biology was sometimes on my side, usually not. Eventually I had a nice dream of my own, about an animal-shaped robot who was loyal to me. And I had another dream about a lake, not Crescent Lake, but a different lake altogether. I'd never seen a lake other than Crescent Lake, but the lake I dreamed seemed so real to me, so real and sharp, that looking at it, in the dream, awakened me. I stood up from the bed and looked down at the blond head of the sleeping girl on the pillow there. Then I left her and walked across the belly hold and up the ladderway, and now I was up on the aft deck, with the black-haired woman, in the dark, fishing for catfish, just off the hard glitter of the city of Port Sisterfield, while the girl Cozilla lay sleeping in the belly hold, the hammer I'd given her tucked under her pillow like a tooth. It was weird how people showed up in one spot and then you (with or without them) showed up in another, plus the other way around. I liked the feeling of the two women being on the boat together, one of them asleep and the other one not, one of them on one deck and the other just below. I liked the feeling, too, of how I was there with them, no matter where I was. It wasn't a bad way to live. There were things to look at, gifts to give and receive, and sometimes the black-haired woman spoke aloud of things she was thinking, her voice both high and low.

—

The black-haired woman stood to reel in the pole she'd rigged for catfish. She inspected the glob of bait in the palm of her hand, opened the spool and let the rig drop to the bottom again. She took a couple of tentative steps back to her chair and I noticed how it was all three toads now, not just the single toad but all three of them, on the deck around her feet, hoping to score meals off the fat pink bloodmoths of her hair. She had to dance around these toads to get from here to there. She sat and the toads hopped in and formed a semicircle around her on the deck. They sat there patiently, like little dogs.

"Take a look," the black-haired woman said, pointing up and out.

I followed her finger. Way up there, on a huge red-glowing guide-wire, which seemed to connect the two lighthouses together high above the surface of the lake, you could see a great long machine come tipping, dangling heavily from the wire. I don't know where it had come from, this sky machine. It was not there and then it was. The red-glowing guide wires, I could see, ran not only between the two lighthouses, but back to the city, too, slanted toward the tallest of the central buildings, on a kind of loop going from rooftop to rooftop, all around the bay. I watched as the great machine, lit up by pink-and-green lights pulsing within it, moved slowly down the guide wire from the top of the lighthouse closest our port side. It was like a whole world on that one line. You could hear music coming from the belly of the thing, thwanging and deep. It was like an animal in the way it inched down the red-glowing cable. Even at that distance I judged the machine to be larger, maybe much larger, than the houseboat *Veronica*.

"What is it?" I asked.

"That's the Hanging Gardens," the black-haired woman said.

—

"If you were the kind of person who set foot on land," she said, "and you'd come to Port Sisterfield on business or for fun, you'd want to go to the Hanging Gardens. It's a famous place, less famous now, I guess, than it used to be. The Hanging Gardens as you can see," she pointed, "is not a boat but a ship of the air. It runs suspended along that cable, back and forth, from lighthouse to lighthouse, and then around the loop and back into the city, and then back out over the bay again from the other direction. It runs twenty-four hours a day. The Hanging Gardens is not a boat, but a cable car, which is a kind of boat, I guess. It's three levels deep, pink in color like you see, and with gold trim, but you can't see the gold trim from here. There's dancing and restaurants and there are sun ones and moon ones and little rooms you can rent. It has a library and it has other things. From here it looks smaller than it really is. It runs back and forth, high over the harbor, picking citizens up and dropping them off."

—

We watched the cable car called the Hanging Gardens shudder down the red-glowing guide wire now, over the bay and toward the far lighthouse.

"The upper level of the Hanging Gardens is open to the weather," she said. "Up on that level there is a nice zinc bar on one end. There's a stage for entertainment, concerts and revenge plays, boy-raffles and singalongs. Upon three of the four corners of the upper deck there are lookout areas, so that citizens might hold hands and gaze over the railing at the lake and at views of the city of Port Sisterfield. In the remaining corner of the upper deck, they've built a small planetarium for the viewing of what goes on in the night sky and beyond, if anything. The rest of the upper deck is given over to a series of gardens." She touched her tongue to the points of each of her seventeen front teeth. "It's where I got the idea to put a garden on the balcony deck of the houseboat *Veronica*, for example. Though the gardens of the Hanging Gardens are much more complex, decorative. There is a garden of ferns and a garden of lush flowers. In the gardens there are many paths. There is even a false creek. There are little bowers and alcoves and statues."

—

She said: "The second level of the Hanging Gardens: this level is fully enclosed, another small bar, this one muted and wooden and thoughtful. There is a restaurant, two maybe, I didn't see all of the second floor when I was there. There is a small hall for the housing, viewing, and selection of prostitutes, the sun ones and moon ones and even more ones. There is a small hotel, with many rooms, where you can sleep for the night, alone or with selected company. There is a library with fine volumes, many of them on witchcraft and carpentry, and there's even a reading room with comfortable chairs and drink service."

—

She said: "But the lower level is the reason to see the Hanging Gardens. It's the reason anyone wants to see the Hanging Gardens. I will wait until last to describe to you the most interesting thing about this lower level. But firstly there is a bar at each end of the lower level, and lounging areas along the length of each of the longer sides. Secondly there is a tasteful hand job stand located centrally, like a little island, right in the middle of the dance floor. Indeed the whole of this lower level is a dance floor. And the dance floor is the most interesting thing about the Hanging Gardens. The dance floor is a glass-bottom dance floor. You can hear the music, now, can't you? The dance floor is glass, and while you dance you can look down between your feet at the surface of the lake, or at the rooftops of the city, or over the surrounding forest."

—

She liked to talk and I liked to listen and she said: "You wouldn't know it, but I used to be a good dancer. But I hadn't come to the Hanging Gardens for the dancing. I'd come because I'd heard that a man who had once called me Trick Witch worked there, running the hand job stand. You can see the name *Trick Witch* in the book of bad names, if you check, crossed out of course. The man who called me that name wasn't anything to me. I'd known him only peripherally, in Torsion Cove, as a man who made small-engine repairs. One night, when I was down-lake at the Oligarchy, the woman Anne Sexton 3 told me that the small-engine repairman had been bragging how I was in love with him, though I was not. The woman Anne Sexton 3 told me that the man had a side job in Port Sisterfield, running the hand job stand on the dance floor level of the Hanging Gardens. The woman Anne Sexton 3 showed me, in a bathroom stall in the men's room of the Oligarchy, how the man had called me Trick Witch, there in his handwriting, and continuing on, some, in small print, about how he had the black-haired woman wrapped around his finger."

—

She said: "I was young then and I had something to prove." She took my hand and held it to tell me this next part. We watched the Hanging Gardens make the far lighthouse, then crank around it on its loop, back toward the city. There were two Hanging Gardens now, one the one I looked at, one the one the black-haired woman spoke of, though both were the same. She said, "So I worked my way out onto the glass-bottom dance floor. I wasn't there for dancing, but it was really something, to look down beneath your feet and see nothing there but the lights of boats on the surface of the lake, all that blackness, like outer space wasn't only above you, but also below." She breathed out deeply and I could feel the wind off the lake blow the warmth of her breath back through me. She said, "The dancers loved this dance floor and they did not wear shoes on it, for fear of harming the glass, but, since they knew their feet would frame the view below, they wore nicely painted toenails, they wore brightly colored ribbon wound around their ankles and toes, some of them even dyed their feet and legs in attractive pairings of color. There were hundreds of them on that dance floor and their bodies all together made it very hot in there, even though, if I remember right, outside it was the midst of Winter."

—

She said, "So I walked my way out into the center of the dance floor, where I knew the hand job stand to be located, and there stood this man who had called me Trick Witch, his back to me. He had a couple of sun ones and moon ones there, the ones he was overseeing at the hand job stand, one of them a pretty boy, I remember, with blond hair, who, now that I think of it, reminds me a little bit of you. The sun ones and the moon ones, they sat at the tables of the hand job stand, waiting for customers to approach them, but everyone was focused on the dancing. I wanted to sit down at the bench next to the pretty blond, to take my time with him, but I wasn't there for such things. The music was loud and it put a little heartbeat in the core of each of my teeth. I tapped the man who had called me Trick Witch on the shoulder and he turned around. He recognized me and I smiled and asked him if he wanted to dance. I hadn't planned to dance or to ask him to dance, it just came out of my mouth. He said yes and he followed me onto the dance floor and we moved together a little bit." She squeezed my hand in the dark. She said: "I'm told sometimes that my dancing can be frightening. And I got a little lost in it that night, I'll admit, looking down at my feet, the lights of the bay beneath me. I even started having a good time. I realized how long my toes were and I forgave them for their length. I danced a little bit against the man who'd called me Trick Witch, despite myself. He stepped back and winked at me and he said, 'I knew you'd be like this,' and this made me angry, the look on his face, and with the tip of my suit knife I found a rib slot, high up near his armpit, and ran it down to the sternum."

A TURTLE

—

"A turtle," the black-haired woman said. She said it and she set the hook. After the story of the glass-bottom dance floor, I'd fallen asleep in my chair. The black-haired woman's voice jerked me awake from whatever dream it was. I don't think I'd heard her say the word *turtle* before. I tried not to think of all the other words I'd never heard her say.

—

She raised the heartbreak-cut green dress over her head. She let it drop to the deck, braced her bare thighs against the rail. The drag growled as the turtle turned for deep water and the *Veronica* turned on its chain as the turtle turned. The pink lighthouse lights crossed and recrossed each other, frosting the black-haired woman's body. Whatever energy I had, whatever thoughts I was having, the black-haired woman's body, there at the rail, powered them. She turned at the waist and looked at me, happy with battle. Sweat stood out on her fragile-looking shoulder blades. It could have gone on forever. I don't know how long I sat there. I thought I should go down to the belly hold to fetch the girl Cozilla, if only to have a witness.

—

"She's coming up now," the black-haired woman said, and at first I thought she'd read my mind and meant the girl Cozilla, but then I knew what she meant, as through the mercury-silver railing I saw the huge moonscape-shell boiling to the surface.

—

She butchered the turtle there on the deck. She put her small foot on the back of the weedy shell and she lifted the fishing pole, connecting by its line to the hook in the turtle's throat, extending the organ skin of the turtle's neck, the nightmare bird-beak snapping left and right for toes. She pulled more and the turtle opened its eyes and the black-haired woman reached down with the pink-handled knife and snicked the head from the tension of the body, the paddle legs still working, trying to find water. She cut the line and flicked the head into the lake and hefted the body so it stood tailside-up on a slant against the rail of the boat. She let the turtle drain from the neck hole, the smell of the turtle like the smell of whatever part of the lake had gone longest without seeing the sun.

—

With her thumb the black-haired woman found the seam where the flesh of the turtle met the cross-shaped undershell and she ran the tip of the knife around the seam. Even though it no longer had a head and was upside down, the turtle kept trying to swim away, though more slowly, like sleepwalking now. Like a lid the black-haired woman lifted the undershell free from its tendons. She arced the undershell into the lake. It made me sad how quickly the turtle no longer looked like a turtle. The black-haired woman pointed the tip of the bone-handled knife at the exposed guts.

She said, "It was about to lay eggs."

—

The black-haired woman pressed the flat of her knife on the still-working gut near the tail. She ran the flat of the knife downward. Out of the grayish tract, one after the other, spilled three oblong eggs, gray and crepe of shell, each egg just a little smaller than the first. The black-haired woman scooped the smallest of the three eggs into the palm of her hand. She stood over the body of the turtle, holding the egg between her forefinger and her thumb, checking it like a jewel. The small moon of the egg between her fingers echoed the larger moon, the true moon, in the sky behind the black-haired woman. I had that feeling where I knew the night all around hid a world much different from the one that was really there. I knew what she wanted me to do before she needed to tell me. I opened my mouth and the black-haired woman crushed the small egg on my tongue.

EVERYONE WANTS TO BELONG TO A WITCH

—

I don't know what your reasons are. I don't know what your reasons are like. Nor how you match your reasons, like a puzzle, to how you behave, nor if they match for real, or you only make them match, or if reason is just a word you travel back in time with, to drop along on the path, how in that way the word connects you to your present, where you are making sensible tea or sharpening your sensible knife. If everyone wants to belong to a witch, then how come so few ever do? It's dangerous, yes. It's a lot of hard work and sacrifice. It's sometimes lonely in the bad way and you'll always long for the togetherness of a death you can't be said to enjoy. There is nothing in the grave and nothing after and in some ways you are a virgin forever. Not even those supplies you bring with you (your teeth and your bone, your meat and ideas) will last very long below ground. Soon enough, the dirt pages through it. No mother and no father, you must be the tree and not the flying thing. You can enter only water and buildings. You might never learn what Winter is.

—

I don't criticize you. The life ahead is hard, yet even worse, full of shadowy things without edge. Take me, for example. Perhaps I had no idea what my reasons were, only lied my way through to them. When I look back on any decision I've ever made, I don't know if

I did any thinking at all. I moved wherever I moved like a magnet drew me there. Tonight, any night, that night. That night, while the black-haired woman and the girl Cozilla lay alone together in the white bed of the black-haired woman's sleeping quarters, why did I, in secret, rise from my bed in the belly hold, creep up the ladderway into the galley and turn my back on the closed door of the black-haired woman's sleeping quarters, then walk past the cockpit and out onto the foredeck beneath the stars, then blow a kiss back toward the closed door behind which the black-haired woman and the girl Cozilla lay, then slip silently into the water of Crescent Lake? Why, with everything I wanted spinning in front of me, with the turtle egg in my stomach and the bolt of meteor in my eye, did I swim from the houseboat *Veronica* toward the nearest lighthouse in the bay of Port Sisterfield, so that I could climb up the rocks, enter the lighthouse, go up those endless stairs to the landing deck and board the cable car called the Hanging Gardens? Why did I wish to see that place which stood for an open world I only wanted to make smaller?

THE HANGING GARDENS

—

There wasn't much wind up there on the upper deck of the Hanging Gardens, but what wind there was didn't make any sense. It batted at you from all sides. You knew the huge metal car must sway on its wire, but standing on it, you couldn't feel it. Or you felt it in a place in the body that the mind couldn't touch, somewhere in the gut or in the heart of the ear. I stood at the balcony rail with the complicated open gardens behind me and I could feel in the railing the vibration of the music from the levels below. Since boarding the Hanging Gardens I'd been trying to make my way across the balcony level to the ladderways I believed would take me down to the glass-bottom dance floor, the source of that music, but—confused by the too-many people and all the new sights—I'd gotten lost in the garden, among the switchbacks and alcoves, the fountains and frog ponds, the random statuary, the here-and-there of the stand-alone lube pumps. Then the garden spat me out at this railing like it wanted me there. The cable car inched us slowly along the wire, the blackness of the lake and the hills surrounding the lake, the bay of Port Sisterfield below. I supposed the city proper was behind us, on the other side. I looked over the rail and tried to see, down into that darkness of lake, the lights of the houseboat *Veronica*.

—

I heard footfall behind me and a woman in a long blue gown emerged from the garden and walked up to me. She had death's-head decals on the toenails of her two big toes. She thought my name was Ricky and she asked me for a lighter. I told this woman how I liked her gown and I said how I didn't have a lighter. She told me how that wasn't very Ricky of me. Then she moved off and a couple, two women, passed by hand in hand, going the other way, matching skirts, matching wigs like beehives. Probably very many of these people would have names they'd answer to. I looked over the railing again. There were many boats down there in the bay, the running lights twinkling green and red in pairs. I picked one of these pairings of light and I told myself it was the houseboat *Veronica*. I told myself how very small it was down there on that boat, the tiny lights, the tiny women I'd left behind. Maybe you couldn't hope to find them again.

—

All around me I could hear glasses clinking and the chime of laughter, whispering and cursing in the garden, queer moans and little cries, a girl in a blue swimsuit puking over the rail, the voice of a single violin, a dog barking, glass breaking, the world opening up. To my left down the rail was a distant slice of stage upon which actors moved in bold costume, the shy upturned faces of the audience. To my right down the rail, past the lovely puking girl in blue, I could see what I supposed was the planetarium, domed like a gold dessert among the manicured hedges, people in fine clothes—many dresses in many strange cuts I didn't know the names of—flowing in and out of the structure, hand in hand. The Hanging Gardens was a little city of its own, four or five times as long as the houseboat *Veronica*, I thought, wider, deeper. There were two more levels that I hadn't even seen. The sky seemed more dark blue than black and I smelled a cold brittle mint in the air and found myself wishing, for the first time, that I owned a shirt.

—

Then an older man wearing a honey-colored costume beard and a neat black suit slipped up to me at the rail and touched me on the shoulder. He must have lost his teeth to the Living Dots, or some other venereal woe, or some kind of violence or accident, because his teeth, now, were not real teeth. None of them were. They were clear glass, and round, like marbles. When he smiled you saw through his glass teeth to the back of his throat.

"And what do you stand here looking at?" the man asked.

He looked over the railing to see what it might be.

"Not anything really," I said.

His eyes were a little foxed around the lids, but he was handsome. He reached into the inside pocket of his suit jacket. "How much for a few minutes in the garden?" he asked.

"Whatever you think is right," I said.

—

The man was complimentary about the pink shorts I wore and then the stitches between my legs. I didn't tell him I belonged to a witch. You never know how people might take that information. He paid not with coin but with bills. When his lower teeth touched his upper teeth it made a sound like music.

—

He found me where I was and where I wasn't and when he was through we sat there, rearranging ourselves on the wooden bench of a little alcove cut into the garden amongst a gang of big-mouthed purple flowers. The man seemed happy. From the direction of the balcony stage came the sound of a round of applause.

"I'm going to pretend," the man said, zipping up, "like that applause is for me."

—

He stood to don his suit jacket and he told me how he liked, afterward, in a garden, to be asked questions. He requested that I ask him something. The man had paid me well and I sat thinking what question to ask him. I wanted it to be a good one. Though in truth I didn't like how much I wanted to please him. I worried it might be in me to hand myself over to this man and just start calling him, in my mind, the black-haired woman. The Hanging Gardens whispered to you how it was possible to belong not just to a witch but to anyone. This was not information that I liked or trusted. Nor did I like it how the girl Cozilla could close her eyes and picture the black-haired woman's face when I could not. There was some failing in me, near the core. Just across from where the man and I sat, there on the flagstones of the path, there was a broken statue of a young boy or girl holding, by the legs, a frog in each hand. At some point the wind or a clumsy merrymaker or the imperceptible sway of the cable car had tumped the statue over to the flagstones, breaking off the head at the neck.

"What question would you like me to ask?" I asked.

"Anything you want to know."

I thought a bit more. The man sat back down.

"What can you tell me about human beings in general?"

His face knotted, loosened. He lit a match and touched it to the tip of a living cigarette he'd produced from his suit jacket. Behind the glass teeth I saw a little tornado of smoke spin on his tongue. Then he started talking to me about human beings. "By and large," he said, "they come from terrible families. They're not sure what to do with their hair. They talk to themselves when they think no one is listening. They like to wear something nice. They pray to invisible entities. Sometimes they write a book. Sometimes they skip meals. They get taller the more they talk. They make and use their own adrenaline. If you ask me," he said, "they seem to have it all."

THE GREAT WHITE QUEEN

—

There weren't too many dancers on the glass-bottom dance floor and I thought the glass of it seemed a little cloudy with wear. It was not the crystal it must have been when the black-haired woman had seen it, seasons and suns ago, but it was still impressive. You looked down and your heart gave in. You thought you'd better hurry up with the power to fly. Below me, framed by my feet, scrolled the docks of the harbor, inching flatly as the cable car rolled toward the city now, boats moving in and out of slips and tiny people in hats on the docks. The music put its heartbeat in my teeth and I made my way over the glass and through dancers, men and women both, with beribboned and dyed feet. I wondered how, when you were dancing, you knew to move one way or not the other. It seemed a complicated thing full of many separate decisions, but the dancers made it look thoughtless and grand. I suspected they practiced their dancing at home. I walked among them and I wondered about their homes, where they lived in the city of Port Sisterfield, how they felt in those homes, how they came to live there.

—

The dance floor took up the entire length of the Hanging Gardens and there was much to look at, and I made my way to the hand job stand, the island platform there in the center of the dance floor where the black-haired woman had once murdered a man who'd called her Trick Witch. The hand job stand was exactly what you thought it might be. The hand job stand was a raised round platform with little love seat benches all along the edges, facing out for a view of the dancing. And built rising from each bench, in the middle, was a little table. The sun one or the moon one would sit on one side of this table, the client on the other. Each little table carried a little stack of napkins and hand sanitizer. I stepped up onto the platform and stood in front of a dark-haired girl sitting there in a pink dress made in what I believe is called the touchdown cut. She was, this girl, the only one sitting on any of the benches. Her eyes rode far apart, like mine. She wore a pink hat with a couple of involved-looking levels to it. It didn't look like a hat that got along well with other hats. She looked at my pink shorts and she said, over the music, "I've not seen you here before."

"I've not been here before," I said.

"That clears up the mystery," she said.

I sat down, not next to her on the bench, but at the next bench.

"It's a nice place," I said.

"It's a good place," she said. "You melt away," she said, "you simmer off."

"That seems right," I said.

"Freelancing?" she asked.

I didn't know what she meant, but I nodded my head. Sitting down, looking out at the dance floor from that angle, you couldn't see the shine of the glass or the scratches at all. The dancers looked like their feet touched at nothing. Waiters in formal wear moved across the dance floor with trays upraised. Mirror balls hung everywhere like fabulous seeds.

"It's a slow night," the girl in the hat said. "We might as well tell each other our names."

—

On a whim I bought a couple drinks from a waiter passing by.

"I made a little money in the garden," I said.

"It's a nice garden," the girl said. She thanked me and sipped at her drink, wrinkled her nose at it. "Though I wish," she said, "they wouldn't plant all the same flowers in all the same flowerbeds. I think it would be better if they mixed the flowers up."

I thought about the gang of open-mouthed purple flowers I'd seen in the garden. "I hadn't thought of it like that," I said.

She nodded her head. Her hat went along with it. "They plant the same flowers all in one spot together," she said. "It makes the flowers seem insecure about other kinds of flowers."

—

"And yet you smell like you belong to someone, Orphan Thing," the girl said. Her name was Madeline. She would turn her head toward me and her body the other way, independent. She seemed built out of swivels.

"What does that smell like?" I asked.

"Like you've had more than one bath."

"I do belong to someone," I said.

"And where is she now?"

"Out in the harbor," I said.

"I like boats," she said.

"I like them too."

—

While we were talking an upright man in a white tuxedo approached the girl Madeline.

"I like your hat," he said.

"It wears me more than I wear it," she said.

The upright man smiled. He had normal teeth. He had some kind of costume beard I'm forgetting the particulars of. He asked her, "What are you doing in a place like this?"

"I'm looking for you," she said. "For you, or someone like you."

The man put an orange coin on the table and sat down at her bench.

"There's nobody like me," he said.

"Then I guess you'll have to do," she said.

—

I watched the dancers for a bit, not looking over at the girl Madeline and the man. I didn't know if it would be impolite to look. The man didn't take long and he left the hand job stand without looking back at the girl, like he had to be somewhere all of a sudden. The girl Madeline plucked a napkin from the stack on the table and wiped her hands.

"That's how it is at the Hanging Gardens," she said.

—

There was a little rush then. Another man sat down next to the girl Madeline. I drank my drink and did not look over. Then a man sat down next to me. I did with him like I supposed the girl Madeline had done. This man didn't take long either and he didn't speak at all. When he left I wiped my hands with a napkin and I looked back over at the girl Madeline. Now she had a woman sitting down next to her. It was the same woman from the balcony deck, the one in the long blue gown who'd called me Ricky. The woman let the girl Madeline see the death's-head decals on her toes and she put a bill and not a coin on the table and she leaned over and whispered to the girl Madeline. Then a beardless man sat down next to me and I turned away from the girl Madeline and toward the new man. Like everyone his feet were bare and colorful. He unzipped shyly and he said, "I tell myself I come here for the dancing."

"It's not such a terrible lie," I said.

—

The beardless man took a little longer and I had to concentrate to get it done. I'd made the mistake of sitting to the right of the built-in table. This made me need to be left-handed. The left hand tired quickly and it went awkward a couple of times and I thought I might have to ask the man to switch places, but eventually the man locked his hand over my hand, finished it his way, thanked me. He stood up and left and I wiped my hands and looked over to the girl Madeline, but she wasn't there anymore. People moved in and out of your life quite rapidly. They took everything but their names away with them. I looked out on the dance floor and saw the girl, just barely, by seeing her hat. She was being led away by the woman in the blue gown, that hat plowing like a schooner through the small crowd. I supposed the two women would search for a nice spot in the garden, or maybe one of the private rooms of the second level, where the hotel was. I felt suddenly very empty and I didn't know what went on between women. The music changed from fast to slow and the dancers paired off and clung to each other like they were floating lost at sea. I stood up and then sat down on the other side of the table, so I could favor my right if another customer should visit with me, and I sat there for a while by myself. I tried not to think about the black-haired woman, what she was doing right now, if she slept next to the girl Cozilla and if either of them dreamed or were pregnant with a baby, but the coin made me think of her, of both of them. No doubt the girl Cozilla was a bride by now. Wouldn't you be? I could think of no reason not to. The coin and bills I'd earned in the garden and at the hand job stand were mine, but I didn't like the weight of it in my pocket. The thread of the black-haired woman's hair stitched the wounds between my legs. She was a tiny dot on a tiny boat, but I took her with me everywhere.

—

Meaning to find the second-level library I somehow wound up on the balcony deck again. Now I stood at the railing on the opposite side of the cable car, or probably I did. We were now wiring over the city of Port Sisterfield itself, it glowing like a furnace as the cable car inched its way above and along, rooftop to rooftop. I turned and worked my way through the garden again, from the other side now, hoping not to get lost in the shudder. I saw how all the flowers, like the girl Madeline said, had been kept

A PROPOSITION

—

Just near the stage was a pretty zinc bar set beneath an arbor over which grew a bright green ivy sending up little yellow flowers. After the performance Anne Sexton 3 and I sat adjacent on two barstools at one corner of this bar. We had the bar corner to ourselves. No one thinks they're going to meet one witch, let alone two. I liked the woman Anne Sexton 3's stage shoes as they were very white and tall like her wig and I told her they seemed made of some material that looked fresh and edible. I hadn't seen many shoes before but I believed these shoes to be serious ones. I liked also the safety of the arbor over our heads as it did its best to cloak the bustle of the balcony deck and I said this to the woman Anne Sexton 3. The woman Anne Sexton 3 agreed with me about the arbor. The woman Anne Sexton 3 added also that she liked to sit at the corner of a bar with someone, as we were doing now, because you didn't have to crane your neck to see who you were talking to. The corner of the bar was a little world for two and you were lucky to get it. It was a special place and the bartender overheard her say this and he was pleased to agree with her. The bartender was the oldest man I'd ever seen and he may have been old enough he wore his own true chin whiskers and I asked him what zinc was and if the bar was made of it. He told me that the bar top was made of hammered tin and the phrase zinc bar more described the type of bar than what it was made of. The woman Anne Sexton 3 said she hadn't known that, and then she ordered for both of us a drink she called the Bowling Ball and it came green and thick in short heavy glasses.

—

The play about the Great White Queen turned out to be a play the woman Anne Sexton 3 had not only starred in but also written.

"Plays when I'm happy," she said. "Poetry when I'm sad."

"I liked your performance very much," I said.

She raised her glass. "You didn't think it too horrible?"

"Not at all. I found the Great White Queen both very forceful and tender as a character. I also liked the clown, who was very funny. I liked the violence and I liked the dialogue."

"You are my favorite critic," she said.

—

The black-haired woman and the woman Anne Sexton 3 were very different witches. The former liked the confines of a boat, the latter liked the open warmth of the stage. There was always going to be too much for me to learn and too little time to learn it. The drink called the Bowling Ball was a strong drink with little flakes of the visionary in it. I was curious as always about how one person could show up in one place and then show up in another. I was curious about how the few people I knew sometimes seemed to also know each other.

"I think you know the girl Cozilla," I said.

"The girl who never met a person she didn't touch."

"That's her," I said. I thought a little. "Do you know the girl named Madeline?"

"I don't think so," she said.

"Big weird hat," I said. "A funny and clever way of talking to you."

"She sounds very nice," the woman Anne Sexton 3 said.

"She was nice," I said.

"It's a large world," she said. "You probably won't see Madeline again." She sipped at her drink. "Nor her hat," she said.

"That's what it feels like," I said. "But then I come through the garden, when I'd meant to be going to the library, and there you are on a stage."

She looked at me, white powder on the tips of her eyelashes. "Sometimes meaningful things don't really mean anything. Sometimes I'm in Torsion Cove, sometimes I'm here."

"And of course you know the black-haired woman," I said.

"We're old friends," she said.

"Have you ever been on the houseboat *Veronica*?" I asked.

She shook her head no. She said, "I won't set foot on a boat."

—

"So you've run away," she said. "Absconded with yourself. And you've accidentally brought yourself to me," she said, "so that I can decide what's to become of you."

"I don't know if that's what it is," I said.

"You think she doesn't know you're here? You think this isn't part of it?"

"Sometimes I know what's part of it," I said.

"And sometimes you don't," she said.

And then she told me a story about parakeets.

It's a story I think about from time to time.

—

"One man I loved," the woman Anne Sexton 3 said, "was a breeder of the bird they call the parakeet. This was an animal, the parakeet, that the man enjoyed very much." From the agreeable old bartender the woman Anne Sexton 3 ordered another Bowling Ball for both of us. Then she said, "This was a troubled love for the man, however, his love of the parakeet. The parakeet is a popular bird, maybe too popular. People keep them as pets, because they're colorful and busy. But people, regular people, didn't understand the complexity of the parakeet, not like this man did. This man understood that one parakeet was not the same as the other. In terms of their wingspan, the set of the beak, the coloration of the feathers, the quality of the feathers, the shapeliness of the skeleton, and so forth. This man knew that somewhere there was a perfect parakeet. He breeds the animal. He knows. He feels it in his heart. To some extent his love for the bird is an aesthetic love. He loves the lines, the angles. He tells me, 'Somewhere there is a fat man, with a fat wife, with fat children. This fat man has just bought a parakeet for a pet.' The man I loved, the breeder of parakeets: it horrified him to think of such a thing," she said. She let one of her edible shoes fall off of her foot to the bar floor and she found the shoe again with her foot. She said, "Somewhere he believed, living with this family of his nightmare, was the perfect parakeet, unrecognized, lost from the bloodline, its wings clipped. It was the waste of it all," she said, "that kept him up at night."

—

The drink called the Bowling Ball was a powerful drink and for a while I only remember time in stunts and flashes. The woman Anne Sexton 3 knew I'd wanted to see the library, and I remember standing next to her in a small leather room overfed with books and smelling the innocent smell of the white powder in her wig. I remember picking up a book the woman Anne Sexton 3 pointed out to me as a fine book. I remember listening to the woman Anne Sexton 3 talk to the librarian, who was a little girl in pigtails and a rubber stamp in her hand and how this girl said with her little voice over and again how it was so very close to closing time. I remember following the woman Anne Sexton 3 down another hall and a ladderway and another hall. I remember looking down, in that hall, and seeing that I held a book in my hand. It was a low-ceilinged hallway and it was a book entitled *A Brief History of Witches*. I remember fearing that, in reading this book, I might run across myself in the history it spelled out. I set the book on a small table in that hallway and left it there. And just then I *did* feel the cable car shifting on its wire, whereas I had not been able to feel its motion before, a weak bend in the heart of the ear. I touched my fingertips to each wall of the hallway and I closed my eyes and felt the earth rolling off.

—

Eventually the woman Anne Sexton 3 led me to the room set aside for her in the small hotel. She sat down on a small white couch and I sat down in a small chair pointed at this couch. She put some orange and turquoise bills on the table between us. Behind her in the room's one window you could see the skyline of Port Sisterfield strolling by.

"We like how you like it but you don't want it," the woman Anne Sexton 3 said. "Or we like that you want it but you don't like it. Or one way or the other. It really doesn't matter."

"Who likes it?" I said.

"You've had too much to drink," she said. "That's my fault," she said. She sighed and looked around the room, her room. The ceiling was low and the shadow of her tall wig tested its height. She looked at me and said, "I hope you're comfortable being in a room that has knives in it."

—

On the walls of her room, I noticed, were photographs of young men jumping nude from tall cliffs.

"I think you don't know how much space you have to move around in. It's limited of course, but you have options, and I think you don't know your options," she said.

I thought she maybe meant the room and how small it was. "I think it's a very nice room," I said.

She crossed her legs and I saw how her legs were not so completely white. It was how she wore fine white stockings. "I don't mean the room," she said. "I mean your murder."

"I never really talked to anyone about my murder," I said.

"You should," she said. "I can talk to you about it if you like."

—

She'd had shoes on, but she didn't have them on her feet anymore. I didn't know where they'd gotten to.

"Your murder is in a lot of different places," she said. "And it might not seem like it, but in some ways it's yours to give. Not everything is yours, yes, not even many things. Not even all of your murder, just parts of it. You're limited in some ways, clearly. You don't have much to call your own and you probably don't want much. But part of the murder is yours. This gives you a certain freedom."

"Where are your shoes?" I asked.

—

About the murder she asked: "I'm right in thinking you mean to give it to the black-haired woman?"

"This is hard to talk about," I said.

"She doesn't want to hurry anything," Anne Sexton 3 said. She gave a brief smile. "A murder like this, between two people who are right for each other, needs to be a careful thing. The timing needs to be right. Of course there is something to be said for rushing it, I won't lie. You let it take you over. You feel a great power. Believe me, I know. But probably it is better for her, in a case like yours, at this point in her history, at this point in the time of one moon and one sun and one sky, to take it slow if she can. She will have had murders in her past that do not, in the present, sit right with her. She won't be wanting to make those mistakes again."

—

She said: "You think she doesn't know this is happening? She's out on the bay right now, waiting to see if you come back."

"You know a lot about it," I said. The blood ran away from my head and I looked at the bills of money on the table between us and looked up at her. I felt fearful but also strong. My murder was on other people's minds. She sent a hand up along her huge white wig and smoothed it, lit a cigarette and leaned back on the couch. I hadn't noticed before that her eyes were gray and I forgot for a second the color of my own eyes.

"Since both minds would need to be right about it," Anne Sexton 3 said, "you can see how this gives you some control. She will be pleased for you to want her to be the one you hand your body over to, but she might not be certain how real you think it all is."

"How real what is?"

She gestured with her hand all around. "Either how real this is, right now, what we're looking at. Or how real the houseboat *Veronica* is. How real, even, you think you are. And saying that," she said, "also leads us to wondering, say, how real you think death might be."

—

"You could run. Of course, you'd be hunted." I opened my mouth to say something but she kept on talking. "Or you could throw your own life away, for example, and not let anyone do it for you. Right up on the balcony level of this cable car, for example, a very steep drop. Or you could get yourself involved in some random sex murder, which isn't very hard to do in Torsion Cove, nor even here in Port Sisterfield. Or you could shop your life around to other people who might be interested in taking it, quickly or carefully, however they tended in their behavior. This would give you some more time to be alive. There are a lot of people like that in the world, looking for someone like you. Not all of them are even witches. But a witch is certainly best," she said.

—

The woman Anne Sexton 3 smiled and showed how her teeth were even and smooth, almost like they were not individual teeth at all, more like bands of coral top and bottom. She said what she was going to say. "Or it could happen here, if you wanted. It won't hurt my feelings if you say no. It could be careful and meaningful. You could stay here with me until we felt it was right. Or it could be rushed and ruined if you liked or if I changed my mind, but again I don't think so. It could be in this room, like I say. It could be full of love or full of all the other feelings."

—

"What are the other feelings?"

"You ask interesting questions," she said. Her wig pulsed white. "Tenderness, I think. Some hatred, though only a sliver. You might feel hate for me too, but I doubt it. You have a kindness about you. Sometimes there's rage for me, but also joy, which is like rage but more clean. You would feel my practice and my care. You'd feel vulnerable. Sometimes there's shame on both sides, but it's fleeting. I never feel guilt until, sometimes, only much later."

—

"Is pain a feeling?" I asked.

"Pain is something you feel," she said. "But it's not really a feeling."

EPILOGUE: RETURN
OF ORPHAN THING

—

Now in the bald and ladylike moonlight the black-haired woman watched the boy called Orphan Thing swim unmurdered toward the houseboat *Veronica*.

She didn't always mean to be drunk. But when she saw his body arrow through the lake from the black rocks on the lighthouse shore, she was glad she was. She didn't like naming all the emotions it was possible to feel and the benzene helped her with this. She'd let a soft part of her mind convince the hard part that she might feel some relief if the boy did not return by daylight, if he ran away, if he leapt from the Hanging Gardens into the bay, if he'd stayed to hand his murder over to the woman Anne Sexton 3. It was a complicated murder in the black-haired woman's heart, the murder of this boy, and she'd never felt clear on it. She thought the boy himself felt clear about it, more clear than she did. She thought it was what he most wanted, even if he didn't know how to describe it. And she even supposed, watching him swim toward her now, that he knew how real it all was, including maybe even death, though you could never tell with boys. She hoped the woman Anne Sexton 3 would've made the boy feel some of the truth of it. It was a thing the woman Anne Sexton 3, good with words, could be trusted with. And now the boy swam his body back to her, to let her decide what was to become of it. But the black-haired woman was not clear in her mind, not even now, and this bothered her. Who would know what death was, who would know when it was, if not a witch? The word *witch* made sense to her less and less. At certain moments in their life together thus far, little moments she couldn't predict, as when the boy turned his profile against the sun, or when he asked a question sideways from his mouth without looking directly at her, or when she stood so close to him that she wondered if he could even see her with his widely set eyes, she felt a sudden impulse to do the murder strongly and quickly. It flashed like lightning in her chest. And without knowing it, she'd find herself rising up on her tiptoes, behind him, the knife already in her hand. At those times it took all she had not to do it. And she would tremble, later, when she was alone, with the lack. And she feared she would only do it, when she did it, quickly like that and without thinking of it, without remembering, without witnessing it. She'd wish then that she'd killed him early on, before she'd named him or had time to think about it at all. And there were other times, too, times when, as she told him a story about the old days and saw the peasant cheer in his face, or listened while he invented some reason she should write a letter to him so he could treasure her penmanship, or when she held his hand or laid her head on his shoulder and felt how much he trusted her, at these times she felt a panic to keep him alive. Was it something in the boy himself? Or just something, as she'd moved further and further into the time of one sun and one moon and one sky, changing inside her? If she did not murder him soon she didn't know how long she might keep him before he slipped off, for real, the way her son had done. She was a witch who'd never been set on fire or drowned. She knew she was the black-haired woman and this was a heavy thing to know. The black-haired woman had a spell that would make your wife swim to the houseboat *Veronica* with her panties in her mouth and she had a spell that would make your husband hairless as a star and she'd had twenty-three brides in her life and she'd had a single son who'd imprisoned himself to escape his love for her and she had a daughter coming quick in the belly of the blond-haired girl named Cozilla, who lay sleeping on the dark boat behind her. The night before she'd sent him to Torsion Cove, she'd looked down at this boy, Orphan Thing, while he lay sleeping against her, the white-blond coin of his hair on the pillow, and she'd felt all the feelings possible, all of them she'd never tried to name, so clearly and all at once, the lightning of the violence, the crash of all the rest. She knew exactly what he was up against. That night she could hear the boy's actual skeleton singing, like it wanted to come out, having hidden too well in a game of hide-and-seek. She'd said aloud to the sleeping boy, her voice tight and small in the sleeping quarters, "Poor thing, you never stood a chance."

—

She hadn't seen him for some hours and when he came out of the water he surprised her with how large he was. In her memory he was always smaller. She knew she was a small person, and she supposed in her mind she shrunk down other people so that they matched her. The boy stood dripping on the aft deck with his shoulders the width of a doorway and he stabbed water from his ear with his pinky and he sat down at her feet to keep his huge shadow off of her.

"I'm sorry I left," he said.

He put the heavy little coin purse on the deck between them. She lifted her foot and pushed its palm against his chest. "Let's not worry about that now," she said.

"Okay," he said.

"Sit there quietly," she said. "I'd like to describe you."

—

The black-haired woman loosed the moths of her hair and they fed from the boy's chest and she watched him watch the moths. After a while he looked up at her.

"Where's the girl Cozilla?" he asked.

"She's sleeping."

"She sleeps a lot," he said.

"In a number of months," the black-haired woman said, "she's going to have a baby."

The boy dropped his eyes. The black-haired woman could see this news of a baby hurt his feelings. She didn't want to hurt him but she liked how unable he was to hide anything.

—

"I had a dream the other night about it," he eventually said.

"Did you?" she said.

"In the dream I'd hoped it would be a girl," the boy said. And he brightened when he said this. She looked again at the width of his shoulders, his chest. She knew, if he stood and took her by the throat, he could murder her nine hundred times. She also knew he'd never do such a thing. She felt protective of him then, and she almost told him to head into the galley for something to eat, and they could talk about it all tomorrow. Instead, she kept her options open. There was still some moonlight left.

—

He said of the girl Cozilla, "I wonder if, now that she has a baby inside, she won't need to touch other people all the time."

"I hadn't thought about that," she said.

"She'll never be alone," he said.

She looked at his simple face and wondered how he came to the strange things he thought. She felt a feeling like hot water in her chest.

"She liked the hammer you gave her," the black-haired woman said. "She keeps it under her pillow."

"I'm glad," he said.

The Hanging Gardens had just started another turn out over the bay, heaving on the wire, and the black-haired woman looked up at it.

"How did you like the woman Anne Sexton 3?" she asked.

"She was very glamorous and kind," the boy said.

—

Finally she asked him, "Would you like to set foot on an island with me?"

"Now?"

"Now," she said.

"I'd like to set foot on an island with you," he said.

—

At some point without her knowing it the boy called Orphan Thing had patched the inflatable raft, and the black-haired woman let him paddle it to the island shaped like a door key, the same island off of which the sister witches had been buried, in the time before the flood, in the time well before the boy called Orphan Thing had been born. She thought perhaps with the sisters close to her the murder might make itself clear, one way or the other. She thought perhaps in the dark of a pine wood and with her feet touching the earth for the first time in a long time she might trigger the calm she'd need to do it the way she wanted to. Plus, she'd once taken another bride there, ages ago, one of the more tender of the remembered murders of her past. He'd been blond, too, like the boy Orphan Thing. She'd met this earlier bride at the Hanging Gardens, the time she'd murdered the man who ran the hand job stand. The boy'd been one of the sun ones or moon ones working the hand job stand. She'd murdered the man and she'd taken that boy with her. When she'd told the story to the boy Orphan Thing, when she'd spoken to him of the Hanging Gardens and the glass-bottom dance floor, she'd left out the part about the blond boy, not knowing why. She wondered if she should tell him now, how she'd buried what was left of that blond boy on the island, the island the boy Orphan Thing now paddled toward. She didn't want to surprise him with what might or might not be about to happen on that island. She wondered if she should say how this blond and early bride had been one of her favorites, how also that she could not now remember the name she had given to that boy, as favorite as he had been, but she kept all these thoughts to herself. She thought she'd remember the name Orphan Thing for a good long while and it was a cold and clear night. The boy sat in the middle of the raft and rowed easily. The black-haired woman tucked her knees up under her heartbreak-cut dress and she sat with her back against the boy's back, he pulling toward the dark lurk of the small island, she looking behind at the houseboat *Veronica* and feeling a cold underbelly to the wind she knew could only mean Winter.

—

"Winter?" he said.

"It feels like it," she said. "You can see how the sky's changed. Maybe not a long one at all. Maybe a very short one."

"Can they be very short?"

"Sometimes just minutes," she said.

"Either way," he said, happy to be saying it, "it's Winter."

—

Night-squirrels lectured from the trees and the boy and the black-haired woman stepped from the raft and walked into the pine forest of the island shaped like a key, the black-haired woman surprising herself with her sure-footedness on land, the tuning-fork hum of the mosquitoes all around.

"There's a nice clearing up ahead," she said.

She let the boy lead them along. He looked back at her from time to time and she thought, by now, that the boy understood what this island was.

"Is a knife very painful?" he asked over his shoulder.

"It's hard to know for certain," she said.

—

He sat on the pine-needle floor of the clearing and looked out over the lake, she guessed, trying to see Winter come in. She believed he sat down very close to the spot where she'd buried what remained of the other boy. She stood behind him and she had the knife in her hand now, but she didn't stand on tiptoe. For all he knows, she thought, these woods around him on this island, and the lake around that island, and the far woods and hills ringing that lake, these are all that exist, and they just go on forever.

—

"Does this island have a name?" the boy asked.

"I don't think so," the black-haired woman said. "Probably on some forgotten map it does."

"Anyway," the boy said, "it was nice to see your feet on land."

She walked around to stand in front of him. "Not many got to see such a thing," she said. She lifted one foot and showed it to the boy. Then she lifted the other.

"Thank you," he said.

"You're welcome," she said.

—

She stepped closer to the boy and lifted his chin with the hand that didn't have the knife in it. She could feel the little flakes of snow hitting against her back now and they swirled all around and she wondered what the boy thought of them. But he was looking, instead, at the knife in her hand. She held it close to her side in hope he couldn't see the hand tremble. If he noticed it, she would say she trembled from the cold. She looked around her at the snow and the dark bowers of the pine wood. She didn't think the Winter would last for more than a night. She thought of the baby and the girl Cozilla. She felt the sister witches at her back. She felt herself both very light and very strong and her knife hand stopped trembling.

—

The boy reached out and touched the hem of her heartbreak-cut green dress.

"Little Witch," he said.

"Thank you," the little witch said. Then she raised up onto her tip-toes. And her heart was very full. And she said, to the boy at first, and then to the moon a little later, "Sometimes it's more lovely than it should be."

ACKNOWLEDGMENTS

—

The opening section—in somewhat different form—was published in *Young Magazine*.

And thank you so much to Fiction Collective 2, Sarah Blackman, and Vi Khi Nao.

And thank you to Case Kerns, Binnie Kirshenbaum, and Jillian Weise for all the help.